T0146603

LORD ONLY KNOWS
A MONTANA MEN NOVEL

BREANNA CONE

LORD ONLY KNOWS
A MONTANA MEN NOVEL

iUniverse books may be ordered through booksellers or by contacting:

iUniverse
1663 Liberty Drive
Bloomington, IN 47403
www.iuniverse.com
1-800-Authors (1-800-288-4677)

ISBN: 978-1-5320-3522-7 (sc)
ISBN: 978-1-5320-3523-4 (e)

Library of Congress Control Number: 2017915605

Print information available on the last page.

iUniverse rev. date: 10/20/2017

CONTENTS

IN LOVING MEMORY OF
CARL J IANNACONE
1952-2013

1

Grant Lord leaned a shoulder against a corner post on the porch of his house on the Double L. It was the only spot available for a solitary moment. Especially since the construction crew had remained on the promise of work in Montana instead of returning to Arizona where everything was on hold for a month or so. His eyes took in the vista before him. The wide expanse of land that stretched as far as his eyes could see had belonged to the Lord family for more than a hundred years, long before he had returned to Centerville to take possession of his legacy. When he had decided to return to the ranch to reclaim the traditions of the Lord family's cattle empire, he also took on the responsibility to make the ranch a success. He was determined to make the Lord Ranch beef once again the best in the nation, which meant he had to keep his eye on the ball, a.k.a. ledger, every single day to keep it from dropping into the red.

The Lord heir pondered the state of his world from a purely analytical standpoint. The cattle ranch was expanding, slowly but surely, according to plan. The occasional construction architectural consult kept his hand in the design business just in case ranching went bust. At the moment, he was working on a plan for a modern day *hacienda* for José Vargas, which was a challenge since most of his previous designs were for high rise office structures or single family homes. But he considered it a labor of love for a childhood friend.

The ranch ledger was flickering around the border line between red and black which meant the profit schedule didn't allow for any changes in the budget. Pinching pennies was a normal state of affairs for a start-up cattle ranch. But if the breeding plans continued to produce healthy steers, he could sell some of the yearlings in the spring, which would provide much needed capital. Capital that would allow for a change to the bottom line.

Then there was his love life or lack of it. His pursuit of Betsy Edwards was going a bit slow. They had not gotten much past the holding hands and necking stage when her car accident last summer had put his plans to marry on hold. The woman's slow recovery from the very serious internal injuries made his usual course of action for courtship inappropriate. Seducing an invalid would have made him a major cad not to mention incurring the wrath of two fathers who kept a close monitor on his amorous pursuit. But, like a true Lord, he proposed anyway. She said yes, albeit unofficially. Betsy had been in the hospital under the influence of strong drugs at the time but he was going to hold the woman to her promise.

I guess two out of three isn't a bad batting average.

With that conclusion, Grant went back inside to join the poker game with the motley crew he called friends. Grant stopped by his office to get a couple of rolls of nickels. No high rollers or serious money needed to ante in with this crew, even if he had it to spare. He retrieved a beer from the fridge and took a seat at the table where Tom Sanders, the three Destchin brothers, and Sonny Lawrence sat in a lively discussion of the correct sequence of the winning hands. The five men were the best construction crew in Phoenix, Arizona and now Centerville, Montana.

"Deal me in. Maybe my luck will change."

This was an overly optimistic wish. The cards were definitely against him this evening. His hands consisted of mismatched suits with no chance of beating a Royal flush or even two of kind. The construction crew succeeded in winning every poker hand.

What was that old adage? Grant mused. *Unlucky at cards, lucky at love.* He hoped it was true. He could do with a bit of luck with his beloved.

When his rolls of nickels were gone, the rancher retired to his office to update his daily log of cattle operations while he still had money in the bank. This update didn't take long since the entries were all expenses. He was staring off into space when Tom Sanders stuck his head in the doorway.

"The boys and I are headed to bed. We plan to walk off José's *hacienda* corners tomorrow and supervise the laying of the drain pipe to get the access road set up."

"Okay. I should have the preliminary draft ready for first review by noon."

"Sounds good. See you in the morning."

Grant thought about the sudden influx of construction work that had occurred with the Ridge ranching crew's inheritance of land and monies from his sister's relative, James Randolph. Her marriage to the Randolph heir ensured the ranch would remain under Mitch's control. Lucky for them, the couple had fallen madly in love, almost from the beginning of the renewal of their childhood acquaintance.

The Arizona contingent had already completed the new riding school which adjoined Jose's plot of land. The crew had stayed on to build the stucco *hacienda* at his request. Except for maybe one of them, who had courtship plans of his own for one of the instructors at the White Family riding academy.

The rancher opened up his architecture software and

checked his basic design. A few tweaks were all that the plan needed. He fingered through the contact spindle on his desk until he found the number for the new Randolph Ranch foreman.

"Randolph Ridge, José Vargas speaking."

"Mercy! You sound almost professional, old friend."

"Do you know what time it is, Lord? It is two o'clock in the morning. Us working folks go to bed early."

"I've heard that before somewhere," Grant replied. "But when inspiration strikes I have to act accordingly."

"I take it you are seeing 'light bulbs' overhead again."

"Something like that. Are you available to check out your new adobe plan tomorrow around noon?"

"Sure. Where do you want to meet?"

"The Sanders crew will be at the house site to check out logistics tomorrow morning so we should get Tom's input, as well."

"Okay. See you there at twelve."

"Goodnight, José."

"Manana, Grant."

Hanging up the phone, the rancher slash construction architect hit SAVE. A big yawn almost dislocated his jaw as he waited for the software to close.

Time for bed, Lord.

At least, I can see my lady love tomorrow. Yeah, along with half of her relatives.

With this thought to occupy his dreams, which were only centered on the positive aspects of his world, the young man turned out the office light and headed up the stairs to the master bedroom.

Grant looked around at the simple furnishings of a rancher's home. Comfortable but no warmth to inspire a man at the end of the day. He knew that Betsy could add a few feminine touches that would make it feel more like a home. He stripped down to his boxers and slipped into bed. He was fast asleep within minutes of his head hitting the pillow. A smile on his face indicated a pleasant dream of the future.

2

The buzzing of the clock on his bedside table was meant to awaken him. He tapped the alarm button to turn off the sound. He had not been asleep, merely resting his eyes. Opening one eye a quarter of an inch, Grant tried to focus on the clock read-out. Six-thirty. Regardless of how late he went to bed, the internal clock of his body sounded a wake-up call the same time each day. Knowing he would not be able to go back to sleep, the rancher headed to the kitchen to put coffee on to brew. A big yawn creased his face as he poured a mug and went to enjoy the sunrise on the wrap-around porch. The sights and sounds of early morning assailed his senses.

The brisk breeze blowing down from the Belt Mountains heralded the approaching winter months, which would make the work on the ranch more challenging. The freak snowstorms Montana was prone to would make it necessary to ride the property daily to make sure the cattle were not tangled up in any brush the storms might blow down overnight. But with any luck the weather would hold off for another month.

When he took a deep breath the smell from the flowers his sister had planted filled his nostrils. The only thing needed to make this moment perfect was if Betsy was there with him. He was starting to get a Betsy fixation but he couldn't help himself. He loved the girl to distraction. And just to think he would never have met her if his sister hadn't moved back to Centerville and he followed to watch over her as he promised their father.

Hearing footsteps on the stairs, he returned to the kitchen. Feeding this construction crew was good practice for when he had kids of his own. He was not one of those men who expected his wife to do all the housework or child rearing. He believed in a fifty-fifty arrangement. And he could always depend on his sister to give cooking advice if he got stuck. Thanksgiving was only six weeks away and he couldn't wait to celebrate with his close friends and prospective in-laws. Just thinking about his sister's roast turkey with all the fixings made his mouth water.

Breakfast was a community affair in the Lord household. While Grant turned the bacon strips in his trusty iron skillet, Tom placed frozen biscuits on a cookie sheet and popped them in the oven. The smell of breakfast cooking soon had the rest of the construction workers invading the kitchen to fill mugs with coffee and harangue the cook about his lack of speed in getting the food ready.

"If you want speed, then you need to make yourselves useful. Those eggs on the counter won't crack themselves."

"I'll do that," Sonny volunteered. "I guess that leaves setting the table for the Apache contingent."

The brothers Destchin crossed their muscular arms over their chests and stared at him. The eldest member of this particular tribe eyed his fellow crew mate "You do know that we have the ability to scramble more than eggs. Right?"

Sonny just grinned at Vitorio then shrugged his shoulders as he pointed to the dish cupboard.

This exchange made Tom laugh and shake his head at their hijinks. The crew teased each other unmercifully but would stick up for their friend in a brawl at the drop of a hat. Sometimes all it took was a derogatory word about ancestry or certain proclivities.

Soon the table in the kitchen was laden with breakfast food with the men digging into the meal with all the gusto of grown men who worked hard to earn their pay. The last biscuit was commandeered by Sonny who slathered it with butter and preserves.

"I deserve the extra calories since I am the runt of the bunch." Another impish grin followed this announcement.

This aside was ignored as Tom cleared the dishes and placing them in the sink full of hot water and soap suds.

"Grant and I cooked so that means one of you has the honor of doing the dishes. Whose turn is it to wash?" he inquired of his crew.

"That would be baby brother Jorge and Bonito is to dry," Vitorio declared.

Sighing as he tied an apron around his waist, Jorge complained. "How can I make love to a woman if I have dishpan hands?"

"Don't worry," Grant told him. "You won't be getting that close to Diane if her sister has anything to do with it."

"I do not know why Nancy disapproves of me so much."

"Probably because she recognizes a Lothario when she sees one," Tom told him.

Jorge shrugged his shoulders at this comment but a certain look entered his obsidian eyes before he continued to scrub the plates and bowls. Soon the dishes were stacked in the dish drain to await the next meal.

The construction crew filed out to the extended cab truck parked on the ranch driveway ready for another long day.

Once again, Tom stuck his head in the office door. The whirr of the design printer sounded in his ears. "We're off, Grant."

"I should be there just as soon as the printer renders the *hacienda* plans," he replied. "While the ink dries, I have to put out the morning hay but that shouldn't take over an hour."

"You know, my friend, you really need another body to work this ranch. It won't be much of a legacy for your children if you work yourself to death before they're born."

"I agree with you but not sure if I can afford the expense right now. Maybe after the first steers get sold next summer."

"I understand. See you later."

While Grant heaved the broken bales of hay in the vicinity of the cattle, he considered his friend's advice. An extra pair of hands would make life a little easier. Sometimes the co-op's bulletin board had hands looking for part-time or weekend work.

I'll make a trip over there in a day or two to check it out. See who is available and what kind of wages they are seeking.

Once he showered and dressed in his favorite worn jeans and chambray shirt, Grant rolled up the blueprint and placed it in a cylinder carrier. He slung the leather strap over one shoulder then grabbed his hat and keys as he left the house.

Although José's property was only two ranches to the west, it took thirty minutes to drive to where the crew was busy shoveling dirt over a metal drainpipe. Parking his truck, the rancher opened the driver's door and stepped out. He propped a foot on the front bumper and scanned the land for the most optical positioning of the building. He nodded his head in satisfaction of the idea that occurred to him. He retrieved the blueprint from the back seat and spread it over the tailgate. Anchoring the corners with large rocks, he called out to the crew boss.

"Tom, you got a minute? I need your input on the placement of the building."

"Sure. I'll be right there."

3

Tom and Grant were consulting the blueprints with an occasional glance at the landscape when José drove up in the Randolph "Mule".

"Howdy," the deeply tanned foreman addressed the men like a cowboy of old.

"Howdy yourself, pilgrim," Grant replied.

"If you two are finished with your bad John Wayne imitation, let's examine this design."

"Don't knock the Duke. Grant and I dreamed of being just like him when we grew up."

Tom looked from one man to the other. He gave them a head to foot assessment "Given your personalities, maybe you should have been watching Cisco and Poncho."

"Did he just insult us, amigo?"

"Si." José grinned at his boyhood friend before he turned the conversation to serious matters. "Where are these drawings of yours?"

The three men stood examining the blueprint for several minutes before José looked up to gaze into the distance.

"Everything looks fine except I would like an enclosed courtyard in front to include a fountain, lots of plants, maybe a stone seat around a tree. A little bit of the old country to remind me of my heritage. And a small stable in the back."

"Okay. That is easily adjusted. I can make it connect to the patio overhang that runs around the building with a covered walkway to the stable wide enough to double as a carport next to the back door," Grant said. "Anything else?"

"How many bedrooms did you plan for?"

"One large master at the rear of the house and three smaller ones on the west side of the hallway toward Centerville."

"Good. That should give guests plenty of privacy."

The rancher gave his friend an amused glance. "*Guests*?"

"Yes. I expect Padre and Madre to visit occasionally."

"Ah. The relatives. I understand perfectly," Grant exclaimed with a wide grin. "Not to mention the occasional female guest."

José winked at the men. "They won't need a separate bedroom."

Tom had been silently observing this exchange but needed more clarification on the actual footprint of the *hacienda*.

"Let's walk off the footage," he suggested. "That will give me a better idea of where to put cornerstones."

José and Grant climbed in the 'Mule' and putted toward the middle of the property while Tom collected the marker flags and distance wheel from his truck. The next thirty minutes passed with the reading of the distances and then rolling down the property to place a flag for reference. Finally, eight flags waved in the breeze blowing down from the Canadian border.

"How does that fit your blueprint, Grant?"

"Perfect. Is that where you want the *hacienda* to sit?"

"Yes. Far enough away from the riding school but close enough to the Ridge for getting to work in an emergency," José said. "I have an account set up at the hardware store. You can order whatever you need and charge it."

Tom nodded his head in acknowledgement of this instruction. "We'll get started tomorrow. With any luck, it will be ready to move into by Christmas."

"We can discuss interior options as soon as we get the footing poured," Tom told José.

"Well, I think you have enough information to get underway so I'll let you get to it." The Ridge foreman climbed back in the 'Mule'. "Call my cell if you have any other questions."

Grant only stayed long enough to roll up the blueprint and hand it to the construction boss.

"I'll get the revised plans to you in a couple of days."

"No hurry. It will take that long for the construction materials to be delivered."

"Excellent. I have an errand to run before I get back to my drawing board."

Grant grinned at his old business partner but didn't provide any clue to this cryptic comment. He hurried to his truck and headed to the riding school. As he drove under the sign that read White Family Riding Academy, he thought about the extraordinary events that occurred immediately after Betsy's surgery. When a blood donation revealed her true parentage, nobody was more shocked than Peter White who embraced his child with all the protective nature he possessed. That was one reason why Grant had proceeded on a slow romance rather than his usual style of courtship. He didn't want to give Pete or Sheriff Edwards, who had raised Betsy as his own for most of her life, any excuse to forbid the marriage.

Peter White and the Bartlett girls were exercising the horses when he turned down the driveway to the riding school. Not wanting to spook the horses, the owner of the Double L slowed the truck to a crawl as he approached the patio. The object of his search was seated at one of the picnic tables going over paperwork with Gwen White. Grant stepped down from the vehicle and eased the door shut.

"Morning, ladies." He included the older woman in the greeting but his smile was for the daughter of the house.

"Good morning, Grant. I was just getting ready to brew a fresh pot. Would you like a cup?" Gwen asked as she slid across the smooth wood to stand.

"Yes, ma'am. Black, please."

Betsy watched as her stepmother entered the house on the pretense of making more coffee. She knew it was Gwen's way of giving them a little privacy. The young woman returned her gaze to the handsome cowboy who slipped an arm around her waist as he sat down next to her on the bench seat. He nuzzled her ear before he kissed her cheek. The adoring look in his eyes was so full of love that it made her mist up for a second. It was incredible to think she inspired that much devotion.

"Hello, there. What brings you to my doorstep this morning?"

"I thought if you weren't busy you might want to ride over to the co-op with me. With winter coming on, I need to hire some part-time help for the ranch."

"That sounds lovely but I have an appointment with the Dean of Studies at UM to discuss the course load I will need to enroll in to make up for losing an entire semester."

"Okay. I guess that takes priority over snuggling up to your fiancé."

"Yes. But not as much fun."

"That's a good thing. I'd hate to have to punch out a professor."

Betsy leaned her head on the broad chest. She could feel his heart beating through the soft material. A deep sigh of contentment eased from her body. A mischievous glance upward through her lashes echoed the smile on her face.

"Professor Janet Evers wouldn't appreciate that."

"You are a terrible tease, my love."

With a gentle finger under her chin, Grant tipped her head up and placed a firm kiss on the lips of his tormentor.

Hearing Gwen's footsteps on the kitchen floor, Betsy disengaged herself and pretended to act unaffected by Grant's ardor.

"How did you plan to get the word out about the job? Are you going to put an ad in the Classifieds?"

Gwen placed the tray of cups and coffee carafe on one end of the picnic table before pouring the fragrant liquid into the mugs.

"What job are you talking about?"

"Grant needs some part-time help on the ranch."

"Will this person need to have ranching experience?" Gwen asked.

"Not really," Grant replied. "The job will mostly be mucking out stalls and putting down fresh hay for the cattle. Keep the water troughs filled. Stuff like that."

"Do you remember Laura Ann Taylor?"

"Isn't that the woman who owns the old sheep property down the road a ways?"

"Yes. Her health has gotten to the point where she had to sell the stock."

"It doesn't sound like she could do manual work," Grant told Gwen.

"Not her, silly." The stunned look she gave the man was filled with disbelief at the absurdity of his comment. "Her grandson just got out of the Army and came to live with her. He hasn't been able to find work."

"Okay. I'll drop by there this afternoon and check him out."

4

The man who wielded an old fashioned scythe on the overgrown weeds in the garden looked up when he heard the sound of a motor slowing to a stop next to his Jeep in the front yard of a typical one-story ranch house. Disregarding the sweat dripping down his shoulders and chest, he turned to retrieve the shirt he had hung on a tree limb. He shrugged into the shirt and waited for the stranger to exit from the vehicle. A sign on the driver's side door read, DOUBLE L RANCH. Since the veteran had only visited on holidays, he didn't recognize the driver who stepped out and calmly extended his hand to the black and white Border Collie who nosed his fingers before he sniffed his boots.

"Heel, Samson."

Grant only caught a glimpse of the jagged scar on the man's bare torso when he had donned his shirt. He watched the dog amble over to sit down at the man's left side before he joined him at the edge of the garden.

"Hello. For a minute there I wondered if your dog was friendly or not."

A hand reached down to pat the head of the animal. "More biscuit eater than attack dog."

Grant stepped forward to extend his hand. That was when he noticed the red scar running from the man's right eyebrow to his chinbone. His hollow cheeks made the scar more noticeable. "My name is Grant Lord, one of your neighbors down the road."

"Jeremy Taylor. Welcome to what's left of the Sheepfold."

"I heard the ranch had closed down. I was sorry to hear about your grandmother's decision to stop raising sheep."

"When Granddad died, it was too much for her, especially after her surgery," Jeremy told him. "Don't mean to sound un-neighborly but what brings you by, Mister Lord?"

"Please, call me Grant. Truth be told Gwen White said you might be interested in a job."

"Miss Gwen is still trying to fix people, isn't she? I overheard Gran telling her that I was staying with her for a while."

Grant nodded his head. "Gwen has a big heart and wants to see people realize their potential. She saved Pete White from a lifetime of loneliness and brought his daughter Betsy into his world to help with his dream of teaching kids to appreciate more than iPads."

"Laura Ann filled me in on all the gossip when I arrived last week," the veteran admitted. "Gran might not get out much lately but the grapevine runs through her telephone daily."

"Keeping up with all the Centerville gossip takes talent."

The cattle rancher assessed the man standing in front of him. Satisfied with Jeremy's clear eyes, he broached the subject of work again.

"I am trying to reestablish the family cattle business on the Double L but find that twenty-four seven isn't enough hours for one man to get all the work done. I need an extra pair of hands to do some of the manual labor. I can only pay minimum wage at this time. Would you be interested in filling the opening I have for a part-time wrangler?"

"Gran needs help in the mornings but I could probably manage four hours in the afternoons."

"Great. You can come by tomorrow and check out the ranch," Grant instructed. He turned to go but paused to look back. "Do you ride horses?"

"Only experience I have with horses is riding in circles on the wooden ones of a carousel ride at the county fair when I was a little boy."

"Then we will have to get one of Pete's riding instructors to give you a crash course. See you tomorrow."

"Thank Ms. Gwen for me the next time you see her."

Jeremy waved goodbye to the cattle rancher then went to tell Gran that she would have to share him part of the day starting tomorrow.

*   *   *

Jeremy Taylor paused at the doorway to check one last time that his grandmother had her medication and a pitcher of water on the bedside table. He also made sure that the walker was within easy reach.

"Gran, I will only be a phone call away if you should need something."

"I'll be fine, Jerry. You go help out that nice Lord boy with his cattle," Laura Ann Taylor assured him. "If you see Gwen White, tell her to come see me sometime."

"I will, Gran."

He was torn between his promise to his father that he would look after his grandmother and the need to supplement his income. Between her social security check and his Army pension they had enough to pay the bills but there wasn't any left over to save for a rainy day. Even a part time minimum wage salary would provide that little cushion needed for emergencies that occurred when you could least afford them.

Since the weather was only a little nippy, Jeremy left

the windows down to breathe in the crisp fall breeze. The large DOUBLE L RANCH sign let him know he was at the right ranch but the smell of cow manure was also proof of the location. He could see the cattle shuffling around the pasture next to the driveway as they searched for a bit of grass to nibble on. The ranch house sat at the end of a long drive where his new employer sat on the porch awaiting his arrival. He climbed the steps and sat down in one of the rocking chairs.

Grant motioned toward the tray on the table between them. "The coffee is still warm if you need a cup."

"Thanks. The caffeine will hit the spot," Jeremy told him as he poured a mug full. "The pain meds I take at night for muscle pain leave my brain a bit fuzzy some mornings."

"Are you sure you can handle a shovel to muck out the barn?"

"Yes. The docs at Bethesda cleared me for physical labor. In fact, they said it would help loosen up the muscles in my upper back."

"What did you do in the Army? Infantry?"

"Nothing so grand. I was a civil engineer. We went in after the fighting to rebuild the villages."

"It sounds safe enough. What happened?"

"Safe enough until we found an unexploded shell inside a building when we went in to assess the damage. We tripped a wire that set off the explosive. The blast dislodged a beam that crashed down into the room. I caught some flying shrapnel. Just a glancing blow but enough to send me back home. The man in front of me wasn't so lucky."

"I'm sure your grandmother is happy to have you here regardless of the reason."

"Yeah. She says it gives her somebody to talk to besides the four walls."

Grant stood and grabbed his hat from the table. "Bring your mug along. I'll show you the barn layout."

Even though the soldier assured him of his physical strength, it was good to see him match him stride for stride as they walked the road to the huge, rambling structure behind the ranch house.

5

Grant swung wide the door of the huge barn which was more like a complex structure of various sections added on through the generations of Lord ranchers. Jeremy could tell that the original barn was little more than a tenth of the size it was now. The side stables were specifically designed to allow the cattle to enter the barn but give the owner access to the center aisle away from all the muck that was soon to be his duty to shovel. A chuckle escaped as he considered that job.

"Forgive me, Grant. I wasn't laughing at the set up. Only that my platoon buddies would tell you that shoveling was one of my many talents."

"That's good to know considering it is a mandatory occupation for a hired hand on a cattle ranch." Grant grinned at the young man who still had a sense of humor after facing a long recovery from war wounds. He stopped to indicate a door in the walkway. "Shovels and other paraphernalia are in this room. There are several sizes of rubber boots so check to see if a pair will fit you."

Jeremy nodded his head before he followed the ranch owner to the end of the barn where dozens of steers were grazing on the hay bales strewn over the ground. The nearest cow ambled up and presented her head. The veteran obliged by scratching behind one ear.

"Are all the steers this tame?"

"All except him," Grant waved a hand toward the

enclosed pen to his right where a massive bull stared over the fence. The animal must have weighted over two-thousand pounds and had a belligerent look in his eyes. "But if you keep a handful of carrots in your pocket, Big Red will tolerate your presence."

"I'll be sure to keep on his good side."

"So, what do you think? Still interested in the job?"

"Yes, I am."

"Okay. Then let's go visit the neighbors."

Back at the ranch house, Grant and Jeremy climbed in their respective vehicles. Grant led the way back up the drive then turned right toward Centerville. For ten miles, the only sight through the side window was fence rows and animals ranging from sheep to cattle. Grant slowed down at the road to Randolph Ridge Ranch but took the first road to the left that ran parallel to the main highway. Due to the dirt surface of the roadbed, he kept his speed under fifteen miles an hour to keep the dust to a minimum for the soldier who followed him.

Just past the paved road that marked the drive to the White Family Riding Academy, he crossed over the graveled covered drain pipe to pull up behind a big Dualie truck and parked. Stepping from his vehicle, Grant waited for his new hired hand to join him. A hundred yards into the field was a shelter made of rough cut timbers.

"I want to introduce you to the crew who are building the new Ridge foreman a *hacienda*. They are also bunking with me at the Double L while the construction is underway so you will probably run into them from time to time."

As he passed the Dualie, Jeremy read the logo on the door. Sanders and Lord Construction. "Are you in the construction business, too?"

"I was in another lifetime. I still design buildings occasionally, but ranching is a full-time job," Grant explained as they joined the men standing under a makeshift shelter. "Guys, let me introduce you to my new ranch hand, Jeremy Taylor."

"Welcome. I'm Tom Sanders, the boss of this motley crew." It was clear from the way the man's eyes lingered on his face that he noticed the scar that was still a raised red welt on the cowpoke's cheek but he didn't mention it.

The slender blonde man introduced himself. "Sonny Lawrence."

Two of the three swarthy men had the new fashioned Mohawk haircut that brought your attention to the high cheekbones that indicated their American Indian descent. The third man had let his hair grow longer and pulled it back with a leather thong. It made him look as if he just stepped off a reservation.

"I'm Jorge and these silent dudes are my brothers, Bonito and Vitorio Destchin."

"Howdy."

The brothers didn't offer a handshake but nodded their heads in guarded acknowledgement of the greeting.

Being of an inquisitive nature, Jorge scanned the man's cheek before asking the question on all the men's minds. "Did you get that scar in a bar fight?"

Jeremy grinned slightly at the young man's bluntness. "No. A fire fight in the desert."

This reply had an instant reaction from the men.

Tom extended his hand. "Thanks for your service, son."

"Have a seat. Would you like a coffee?" Vitoria asked.

Jeremy looked at Grant. "Do we have time, boss?"

"Of course. The riding lessons at the academy can wait a few minutes."

This information caught the attention of the youngest Destchin, who frowned. "You are going to learn how to ride horses?"

"Yeah. Jeeps and tanks I can handle but horseflesh is a mystery and Grant assures me it is part of the job duties."

"I thought *Nancy* might have time to do a crash course," Grant told the men. He had to smile at the immediate relief on Jorge's face.

The men talked for a few more minutes then Grant tossed his empty cup in the trash bin. "We better get going, Jeremy."

"It was good to meet you. See you around the ranch."

"I almost forgot," Tom said, "Kris is feeding the crew dinner. And since she cooks better than you, we accepted her invitation."

The next leg of his new career journey was a short one. The riding academy was right next door to the new construction site. Following the boss's lead, Jeremy parked his Jeep next to a corral and walked to the fence to gaze at the two women who were exercising several horses. They were both in their early twenties with light brown hair pulled up in a ponytail. They wore Western hats and cowboy boots. Similar facial features indicated that they were related but one had incredible hazel eyes. One minute they appeared blue, the next green with brown flecks, a veritable kaleidoscope of colors that fascinated him. He was even more captured by their ever changing hues when his boss called her over.

"Nancy."

The woman rode the black mare with white streaks in its mane to the fence and dismounted.

"Hello, Grant. Is this my new student?"

"Yes. This is Jeremy Taylor. Nancy Bartlett, one of the Academy's riding instructors, will get you up to speed."

"So you want to learn to ride a horse?"

"Grant tells me I do. Hopefully, you can teach a

greenhorn enough to stay in the saddle rather than in the dirt."

"I think I can manage that. I'll be right there."

Nancy walked her mount to the gate to exit the corral then led him to where the two men were waiting.

"Betsy is working up the next session's schedule if you want to visit her while I acquaint Jeremy with his new friend."

"I like that idea. I'll wait in the main house in case I need to rush my hired hand to the hospital."

Jeremy gave Grant a strange look but addressed his next comment to his teacher. "Who's Betsy?"

"Grant's fiancée and the daughter of my boss, Peter White."

"I see. That's how we ended up here instead of Grant showing me the ropes, so to speak."

"True," Nancy replied before she motioned him to the left side of the horse. "You mount a horse from the left side by grabbing hold of the saddle horn and the reins or part of the mane, place your left foot in the stirrup then hoist yourself into the saddle by swinging your right leg over to land your butt in the saddle. Like this."

In one lithe motion, she vaulted from the ground to the horse's back. Then she dismounted with the same grace. "Now it's your turn."

"I'm game."

While Nancy held the bridle, he tried to follow her instructions. It was not a pretty sight but he managed to not fall off the other side.

"Not to worry. You'll get better with practice. Are you ready to chance a ride?"

"Maybe. There isn't a steering wheel. How do I make him go where he should?"

"I'll help with that. If you move your left foot, I'll mount behind you."

Jeremy nodded but was unprepared for the rush of adrenaline when she settled her body next to his back as she reached around to take the reins in her hands. The warmth of her body created emotions he hadn't experience in a long time.

"Give him a slight nudge with your heels and he will start a slow walk."

"Okay. I hope you know what you're doing. Here goes."

The nudge did exactly what Nancy said. The horse headed to the barn a few yards away. The rhythmic rocking of horse was a little alarming but his teacher held the reins in firm hands. As they neared the open doorway, the horse responded to the tug of the reins by the woman. A terrier mix watched from atop a hay bale as they reached the shadow of the barn breezeway.

"Who's your friend?" Jeremy asked with a nod at the dog.

"My old pet who assumed he was welcome when we brought our mounts to the Academy stable. No worries. He is as tame it gets." Nancy scratched behind the ears of the dog before she turned back to her student. "Hold the reins steady while I dismount."

Again Jeremy nodded his head as he gripped the leather straps in a white knuckle grasp.

"Now, you dismount the same way you got on. Right leg over his withers to touch the ground then remove your left foot from the stirrup."

Jeremy did as told as carefully as he could. He did not want to embarrass himself the first day.

"That wasn't so difficult, was it?"

"No. It just felt strange to be up in the air with only a tenuous hold on a massive beast."

"That's all for today. As soon as I unsaddle Cruella, we'll go find Grant."

"Cruella is an unusual name for a horse."

"Yes. We took it from a Disney movie. The kids love the odd name and it is easier to remember than horse # one, two, three, etc."

"Makes sense."

6

Grant and the academy owners were letting their coffee cool a bit when Nancy and Jeremy approached the patio. From their startled expressions, the veteran knew they noticed his scared face. Funny thing was he hadn't seen that reaction from Nancy. She treated him like he was as normal as any other man. Maybe he had been so awed by those eyes, he didn't see anything else.

"Pete, Gwen, this is my new hired hand, Jeremy Taylor."

Ever the gracious hostess, Gwen stood up to walk toward him. Thinking she would shake his hand, he was surprised by the warm hug she enveloped him in.

"Welcome home. Your Grandmother Laura told me you were staying with her for a while."

"Thank you, Mrs. White," he answered. "It is good to be back in Montana. Gran said for you to drop by anytime."

"I'll try to do that soon," Gwen replied. "This is our daughter, Betsy Edwards, the brains of our outfit."

"Gran has filled me in on the news of the area. I hope you are recovering swiftly from your automobile accident."

Betsy shook her head in resignation. It was disconcerting to have your innards discussed by all the neighbors. "I'm doing well. And I see you are, too."

"That I am."

From the frown between his hired hand's eyes, Grant suspected the subject was making him uncomfortable.

"Help yourself to coffee," Grant invited. "Then tell me how your riding lesson went."

Jeremy strolled to the serving cart next to the open doorway of the house. He poured a mug full then rejoined the group at the table.

"I managed to stay on top of the horse but not sure how competently I accomplished that feat."

"Jeremy did fine for the first lesson. He will be a good horseman within a few weeks."

"That bad, huh?" the man joked but was secretly happy to know he would see the riding instructor again. Hopefully, sooner than later.

Grant joined his hired hand at the end of the picnic table. "We'll let you entrepreneurs get back to business."

"Damn, the boy is using fifty cents words today," Pete joked.

Arching an eyebrow, the rancher retaliated. "I know some ten cent ones, too, old man."

"Don't insult your future father-in-law, son."

"Pete, behave," Gwen ordered. "Forgive the family discord, Jeremy. They are only teasing one another."

"No need to apologize, ma'am. It is nice to hear an exchange that shows an expression of love and respect. That is the only thing I miss about the Army."

Grant put a hand on the boy's shoulder and turned him toward their vehicles.

"Nancy, give this comedian a call when you have time for another lesson."

"Sure. Maybe day after tomorrow around ten?"

"I'll be here."

Nancy smiled at the new riding student. "See you then, Jeremy. Have a nice day."

Jeremy's sense of humor made him grin broadly. "Since my job is shoveling…muck, I'm sure it will be delightful."

Pete waved goodbye then turned to his wife. "I like that boy. He hasn't let life destroy him."

"Me, too," Nancy added her bit to the conversation.

Pete's protective side kicked in immediately. "Now, girl, you just met the man. Don't make any hasty decisions."

"I'll be careful, Papa Pete." The riding instructor blew him a kiss before she sprinted to the barn.

Gwen and Pete stayed on the patio to enjoy their coffee while Betsy went to the office to work on the Spring session's paperwork.

Grant made one more stop on the way back to the Double L. Jeremy dutifully followed his boss down the next driveway and parked behind him when he reached the large barn with "THE RIDGE" painted on the doors in bright red letters.

"Come on, Taylor. I want to introduce you to the rest of my family."

Inside the dimly lit passageway, the men stopped at the front stall. Grant looked around what appeared to be an empty barn then hollered loudly.

"Kristy, you here?"

A disembodied voice answered from somewhere nearby. The mistress of the ranch was checking on one of the horses.

"Be there in a second. Wearing my vet hat this morning to examine one of the mares who is in gestation with another Black foal."

When the stall door opened and the vet stepped out, Jeremy had to do a double take. He had not realized that the boss's family consisted of an incredibly beautiful woman. You expected a female vet to be a large big-boned woman with harsh features. Despite the faded jeans and grubby gloves she wore, the rancher's sister looked like a fashion model as she strolled down the barn aisle.

Grant kissed his sister's cheek but kept his distance from the gloved hands covered with some unknown substance.

"Kris, this is my new hired hand, Jeremy Taylor."

The woman stripped off her soiled gloves and extended her hand. "You must be Laura Ann's grandson."

"Yes, ma'am," he replied. He forgot just how fast small town grapevines worked. "It is clear to me that you got the looks in the family."

"Did I mention that Jeremy's job is to shovel the stalls?" Grant gave his hand a glare in reaction to this playful remark.

"Don't mind, my brother. Even though I have my very own Montana cowboy to fend off blarney, he still wants to protect his little sister."

"Tis no blarney, ma'am." The twinkle in Jeremy's eyes belied that statement. "Just speaking the truth."

Kris and Jeremy ignored the derisive snort from the cattle rancher.

From the back of the barn, the jingling of spurs announced the arrival of two men. The taller one smiled at the woman who returned the look with such love that Jeremy regretted flirting with her, even in jest. The smaller man's dark complexion proved his Spanish ancestors had made it to the North Country at some point in time.

"Kris, what is the 'brother' up to today?"

"He has hired some ranch help and wanted to introduce him to us."

Jeremy stepped forward to shake the horse rancher's extended hand and prevent questions about his scarred face. "Good morning, sir. I'm Jeremy Taylor, formerly of the Fifth Battalion, Afghanistan."

"Mitchell Randolph, soldier. Glad you survived the battle." Mitch motioned to the man standing behind him. "This is my foreman, José Vargas."

"Mr. Vargas."

"Por Dios! My father, he is Mr. Vargas." The man's heavy Spanish accent dropped away as he spoke again in a normal Western twang. "Call me José"

Grant let the men bond for a minute or two then touched the hired hand's shoulder. "We better get back to the ranch. Your shovel awaits."

"It was good to meet you, Jeremy," Mitch said. "Don't let Grant work you too hard."

The drive back to the Double L didn't seem as long as it did the first time, which happens when the route is familiar. After collecting the rubber boots, pitchfork, and wheelbarrow, Grant told the hired hand to empty the muck into the large compost bin at the back of the barn.

"Do you have a cellphone?" At Jeremy's nod, the rancher handed him a business card. "I will be out checking the herd but call me if you have questions."

"Can't be that difficult to scoop, deposit, repeat."

"It isn't." Grant grinned at the man. "Take as many breaks as you need to if your back gets tired. No hurry. The job doesn't have to be finished today. It will still be here tomorrow."

"Okay. I got it under control." Jeremy assured him but wondered about the truth of that when he opened the first stall and the stench of manure filled his nostrils.

7

Grant saddled his horse Buckshot, and prepared for a long afternoon of riding the boundaries of his property. Truth be told, he used the solitary time to contemplate life and other things like the state of his cattle ranch. He knew the future would be okay, but unlike construction work, the results or income were not always immediate. Slow but steady was the normal progress for raising livestock of any kind. His woolgathering was interrupted when he spied a calf tangled in some brushwood. He dismounted and extracted the heifer without too much effort. A check of legs revealed only minor scratches. With a slap on her rump, the heifer scampered off in the direction of the other cattle.

The rest of the afternoon was uneventful. The fences were all still intact. When Grant reached the back forty corner post, he tied up his horse, gave him a drink of water from the canteen, and slid down the post to enjoy some jerky. This small snack created a sense of well being that made him lower his hat over his eyes and cross his arms over his chest for a quick twenty winks. The sun had dipped behind the tree line when a buzzing sound awoke him. He reached into the breast pocket of his denim jacket.

"Double L."

"Grant, Jeremy. It's five o'clock and I was getting ready to go home. Do you need me to stay until you return?"

"No. That's fine. How are you feeling?"

"A little exhausted but it's a good tired."

"See you tomorrow afternoon. You might throw in a large handful of Epson salt in some hot bath water. Works wonders on strained muscles."

"Thanks for the advice, boss."

Grant mounted Buckshot and finished his inspection of the property. Reaching the trail that led to the barn, he let the horse meander along. They had made this trip so often his horse knew the way without any prompting from his rider. The buckskin knew a bag of oats was waiting at the end of the ride. Like Buckshot, Grant was ready for something more substantial than beef jerky.

The rancher dismounted in the center aisle of the barn, rubbed down the Palomino, then filled the oat bag strapped to the door of his stall. Satisfied that the horse was taken care of, he proceeded to attend to his needs, as well. First, was a shower; second, the creation of one of his sister's inventions, a triple-decker stacked sandwich, washed down by several cold beverages, a.k.a. beer.

Tossing his empty bottles into the recycle bin, Grant was building a fire to combat the slight chill of the evening when his cell phone rang.

"Double L."

"Hello, Grant. How is my favorite brother?"

"Evening, Kris. What's up?"

"What makes you think anything is up?"

"Usually, when you wax sentimental, you want a favor."

"I am seriously offended at the accusation," she stated but when silence greeted this rebuke, Kristy continued. "I wanted to get your opinion on the Thanksgiving meal."

"My opinion is that I like to eat it. Come on, out with it."

"I guess you know me too well, big brother. The guest list is my real question."

"Okay. Go on."

"With the construction crew staying with you, I think they should be included or at least invited."

"I agree and they will most likely accept any offer of free food. So what is the issue?"

"Table space. I don't really have a place to seat eight people. Any suggestions?

Grant pondered that for a minute. "Since the three neighboring ranches and their owners are related in one way or another, why not ask Gwen and Pete if they might consider providing the table?"

"They do have that huge academy dining room table that would certainly be large enough," Kris admitted. "One big happy family celebration sounds like a wonderful idea. Thanks."

"You're welcome. Any other problems you need me to solve?"

"Not at the moment. Talk to you later."

The cattle rancher settled down on the sofa to watch the flames jump. It must be a throwback to cave days but a fire crackling in the fireplace seemed to calm his soul. Because he had solved his labor problems, he let his mind dwell on the future he had planned with one Betsy Edwards-White. By the end of spring, she would have finished the last semester of college. That left setting a date for a wedding if the cattle sales went as he hoped.

Closing his eyes, he imagined what life with a wife could be like. Waking up in the morning with her beside him in bed, kissing her goodbye before heading out to the pasture then coming home to her at the end of a long day. It sounded like pure heaven. When a huge yawn erupted over his face, he set the screen in front of the burning embers and took himself to bed to dream of the future.

After breakfast the next morning, Grant went to the barn and began to saddle up Buckskin when his hired hand drove up. The rancher waited for Jeremy to step out of his Jeep.

"Morning, Jeremy. Have you decided the work is too much for you?"

"No. Nothing like that. Gran has a doctor's appointment this afternoon and I wondered if I could swap hours?"

"Sure. Works for me."

Together they walked down the barn aisle to where the pitchfork and rubber boots rested in the wheelbarrow. Grant tugged on Buckskin's reins and he followed behind them.

"Did the three stalls I finished yesterday meet muster, boss?"

"They did. I will be checking the herd for a couple of hours but should be back by noon."

"See you then."

Jeremy watched the rancher vault into the saddle and guided the horse through the gate that opened automatically when he approached. It seemed that the cattle ranch had been updated to eliminate the need to dismount and unlatch gate fastenings. Maybe he could suggest some more updates to make it more efficient.

By the time Grant returned, Jeremy had three more stalls cleaned and fresh hay strewn in them. He was dumping the soiled hay in the compost bin when the Palomino and rider approached the gate.

"How does that gate work? Automatic eye or remote?"

"Remote. I wasn't sure an automatic eye could withstand the harsh weather we have in these parts."

"Did I mention exactly what I did in the Army?"

"No."

"I was part of the civil engineering unit. We didn't reinvent the wheel but we came up with some new ideas that dealt with the heat of the desert region."

"Okay. What does that have to do with cattle ranching?"

"Well, it doesn't look like there are enough stalls to hold all of the cattle. When your herd increases, it will get more crowded."

"True enough but my bottom line doesn't allow for expansion of the barn right now."

"Understood but I might have an idea or two that could deal with the overflow without costing an arm or a leg."

"If so, I would love to hear them."

Jeremy looked at his watch. "I need to pick up Gran right now. Let me draw up a plan tonight and present it for consideration tomorrow."

"I look forward to hearing this plan."

"See you then."

Grant's eyes followed the man as he drove his Jeep down the driveway. It appeared he got more than manual labor when he hired the veteran.

8

The next morning revealed a score of stiff muscles when Jeremy reached over to tap the button on the alarm clock. Despite the physical discomfort, he was looking forward to his morning riding lesson. However, horse handling prowess wasn't the center of his excitement. The White Family Riding Academy instructor was the first woman who had not turned away in repulsion at the sight of his marred face. His high school sweetheart took one look and never returned to the rehab hospital. That fact created yet another scar. But this one was internal and still smarted when he thought about it. Shaking off the memory, he pulled on worn jeans and an old army T-shirt then contemplated the available footwear in his closet. Sneakers and dress loafers but not the usual cowboy boots that horse riders used. That only left his Army tactical boots sitting on the top shelf, a relic of other days. Not ideal but better than sneakers or shiny shoes would be. After lacing them up, Jeremy went downstairs to help his mother fix their breakfast of eggs, bacon, and toast.

While the bacon cooked, he broke a dozen eggs into a bowl, added a splash of milk, and began to whisk them into a frothy mixture. His grandmother sat at the kitchen table sliding slices of bread into the toaster slots.

"I'll take three this morning, Gran. All this exercise has sparked my appetite," he said with a crooked grin. "I'm sure I can work off the extra calories."

Laura Ann nodded as she happily added another slice to the toaster. The exercise had also added more color to his face. Working outdoors in the sunshine was a big improvement to the body and mind of her grandson. His eyes showed a zest for life that wasn't there when he arrived two weeks ago, battered and discouraged. She would make a point of calling to thank Gwen White for suggesting her grandson to Grant Lord.

Jeremy Taylor parked his Jeep next to the patio at the end of the White Riding Academy road and walked up the paved path to the house. Seeing Mrs. White puttering around the kitchen, he tapped on the open door.

"Morning, ma'am."

The woman turned and observed her visitor. "Good morning, Jeremy. May I help you?"

"I'm looking for Nancy who promises to make me into a cowboy worthy of the title."

The slight tug of his smile made her own face answer in kind. "I did hear about that project. Nancy is at the barn."

As he turned to go, Gwen offered a suggestion. "Real cowboys wear sweat stained Stetsons not camouflage caps. I'm sure Nancy can find suitable head gear."

"Thanks for the advice. I definitely need to look the part," Jeremy answered with a gleam in his eye.

His grin made her chuckle.

The Army veteran had faced many dangers but the uncertainty of the current situation had his stomach tied in knots. As he approached the open barn door, he observed his riding instructor currying a big roan, whose expressive eyes revealed his appreciation of the woman's efforts. He must have stepped on a twig because the animal threw up his head to check the direction of the noise.

"Whoa, boy." Nancy grabbed the bridle. "I see you didn't give up."

"No, ma'am. No quit in this soldier."

"That's good to know. Are you ready for the next lesson?"

At his nod, she walked the horse to the stall and looped the reins around the top plank of the stall.

"First we get the horse used to your scent," Nancy told him. "Hold your hand palm down up to his nose."

Obeying her, Jeremy cautiously extended his arm and waited while the roan sniffed his skin then nudged his fingers.

"Does that mean he likes me?"

"Either that or he wants a sugar cube," Nancy advised with a twinkle in her eyes. Reaching into her jacket pocket, the instructor handed the sweet treat to her student. "Hold it in your palm and he will lip it off."

Even though Jeremy was a bit cautious, he did as he was told. The feel of velvety lips on the sensitive skin of his palm tickled a bit and made his fingers flex instinctively.

"Okay. Now we progress to the next step. Saddling up. First, the blanket goes in the center of the back."

The veteran accepted the wool blanket, placed it on top of the huge animal, and smoothed out the fabric. "Next."

"Put the left side stirrup over the top of the saddle then gently put it on top of the blanket."

If Nancy had not been looking closely at his face, she would not have noticed the tightening of his brow and slight grimace. Knowing he wasn't likely to accept help with such a simple task, she waited until the leather settled onto the horse's back.

"You okay?"

"Yeah. All this manual labor has the back muscles a little tight," he replied but the smile he offered her didn't quite make it to those expressive eyes. "What's next?"

"Now, you retrieve the stirrup, reach under the belly to locate the cinch strap and inset it into the hasp."

"Cinch strap? Hasp?"

"Yes, that stretchy thing that has to be placed in the metal ring then tightened to make riding safe."

Despite the obvious pain he was feeling, he chuckled. "Safe is a relative term to a soldier."

"Safe is making sure the saddle doesn't slide around the horse and you wind up sitting in the dirt."

"Understood." Glancing under the roan's belly, he pulled the strap over to the hasp, threaded it through, and pulled it until it was in the correct position.

"Give the saddle a tug to see if it is snug."

Taking the saddle horn in his left hand, Jeremy pulled. "It seems okay to me."

"Good job. Now take your shirt off."

"I beg your pardon?" The look of incredulous surprise he gave the woman was full of wonder and hope.

"When the academy mounts have a muscle strain, I apply liniment. It will help those achy muscles of yours, as well."

"I'm not sure I appreciate the comparison to an animal."

"If it makes you more comfortable, think of yourself as a stallion or stud."

Jeremy chuckled under his breath and knew his cheeks were probably a deep red. He removed his jacket then his T-shirt and presented his torso for her inspection. His chest was nothing out of the ordinary; just the usual spattering of chest hair but the back was another matter. A slow turn revealed his fortunes of war. Or misfortune to be more accurate.

"Sit on this hay bale. I'll get the salve."

Soon his riding instructor turned therapist returned from the tack room.

"My hands are a little chilled but the liniment will warm up the area very quickly."

"That would be appreciated. A man could get hypothermia posing half-naked in the cold temperatures today."

"Relax. It won't hurt much, I promise."

Jeremy rolled his shoulders to ease the natural tension of waiting for her reaction to the jagged scar left by hot shrapnel. The gentle pressure of her fingers as they spread the cooling gel made him take a calming breath then suck in a gasp as Nancy applied more pressure to the area. The sensual feathering changed into deep tissue massage that chased away any thoughts of pleasure.

"Your therapeutic methods remind me of a drill sergeant I used to know."

"The horses never complain. They seem to enjoy the attention."

Jeremy decided to ignore the obvious reply that surfaced on the edge of his mind. There was attention then there was *attention.*

As Nancy continued her ministrations, the veteran felt the first wave of heat penetrate his shoulder and the muscles began to respond.

"Just to counterbalance the strain, I am going to apply the salve to the left side. As soon as you feel the warmth, flex your muscles to loosen up the entire back."

Jeremy closed his eyes and breathed in deeply as he waited for the desired reaction. Turning his shoulders from front to back he began to notice that the wound didn't pull as much as before. He closed is eyes to let the sense of touch be the only feeling he experienced.

"Aah. That feels wonderful."

"I bet it does," an amused male voice said.

Jeremy's eyes popped open to see the academy's owner standing in the barn door observing them. Peter White was not sure what was going on but he didn't make another comment.

Nancy looked her boss square in the face before she replied. "I thought a little TLC would hasten the training session if the sore muscles were relaxed a bit."

"Don't mind me. I just brought some carrots for the horses."

As he walked by them, Pete glanced back. His eyes widen in shock as he saw the wide red welt on the soldier's bare back. Understanding why Nancy was tending to the wound, he patted her shoulder in silent approval.

"I think that last massage did the trick," Jeremy told his masseuse.

"Okay. You can redress then the fun begins."

After pulling his T-shirt back over his head and donning his jacket, the veteran turned to face his instructor who was wiping the liniment from her fingers before handing him the roan's reins.

"You are one odd female."

"I'll take that as a compliment." Nancy plucked a weathered Stetson from the barn door rack and offered it to her student. "Time to mount up, cowboy."

9

Since shoveling manure didn't require much concentration, Jeremy's mind returned to his riding lesson that morning. When Nancy asked him to remove his shirt in the breezeway of the barn, that same mind leapt to what could have been a more pleasant interlude. The natural stirrings of male awareness reminded him that it had been over two years since his last sexual encounter. Instead, the woman had only wanted to apply the liniment salve that he could still smell over the aroma of the cattle barn. He had to admit that the woman had magic fingers because his back muscles were less painful than they had been since he left the rehab center. Seeing Grant returning from his afternoon ride, he pushed the wheelbarrow to the compost bin.

"Howdy, boss."

"Howdy." Grant's mouth crooked up in a slight smile at the comic delivery. "You seem to have been especially busy today. The bin is almost overflowing."

"Oh, yeah. The cattle are very prolific in their output," his hired hand answered. "Do you have time to look over my plans?"

"Yes. Rinse off those boots and join me on the porch for a cold beer."

Jeremy did the request one better. He changed the rubber boots for his tactical ones because no matter how much water you used, the work boots retained the odor of livestock manure. He didn't need any distraction as he discussed his ideas with the boss. Sitting down in the empty rocking chair, he picked up the beer bottle, twisted the cap off, and took a big swig before he opened the sketch pad to reveal the type of lean-to he had drawn.

"As you can see, it is just a rough idea of a structure that will allow the cattle who don't seem to like being indoors to have a shelter of sorts on the days when rainy or snowy conditions make staying in the open hazardous."

Grant examined the sketch for a few minutes before he spoke. "What are these areas at the back of the lean-to for?"

"Water and feed troughs that we would have to fill on a daily basis. The size of the structure can be any dimension you need."

"What materials did you have in mind?"

"Rough lumber for the framework, the wider the better, on three sides, and part of the fourth side, galvanized tin for the roofs. Thick plastic sheeting strips could be hung on the rest of the front side for easy entry into the shelter plus provide some protection from the wind."

"As a fellow architect, I like the idea. I will pick up the needed materials in the morning and we can build a medium size shed as an experiment. If the cattle make use of the shelter as we hope, we can put more up in the outlying pastures."

The two men spent another half-hour discussing the size requirements and an ideal location before dusk began to fall.

"Shoot, I meant to do a little more work before I quit for the day," Jeremy told Grant.

"That's okay. This was valuable time spent working out the plan. See you tomorrow, bright and early. This project will take several hours to complete."

He watched as his hired hand walked to his Jeep and waved a hand in farewell as Jeremy drove away. It seemed like the veteran and he had more in common than he realized. This lean-to plan was efficient and practical. Grant settled back against the chair and sipped his beer as he visualized the construction project and the materials he would need. When his eyes began to droop, the rancher roused himself to shower and fix a meal before he tweaked the lean-to plan just a little.

Grant allowed himself a quick meal of soup and a hearty roast beef sandwich then went to scan the vet's plan into his software program. He wanted a formal design in case Jeremy decided to patent the lean-to. It had a lot of merit. Back forty ranch pastures had need of animal shelters when the weather turned nasty in all areas of the country. The man deserved first shot at any profit that could result from public distribution. The rancher worked for an hour or so before he was satisfied with the plan. He saved the design and closed the program when the clock chimed ten o'clock. Grant only hoped his brain would turn off so he could get the sleep he needed for the next day's agenda. There would be a lot of physical exertion needed to make this project a completed building.

* * *

For a second or two after he tapped the snooze button, Jeremy couldn't remember why he set the alarm clock thirty minutes earlier than normal. Yawning wide, he swung his legs out of the comfort of the bed to put on jeans and a T-shirt suitable for more manual labor than he had done since before the injury occurred. With any luck, his personal masseuse would offer to treat any extra muscle strains he endured at the next riding lesson.

When he told his grandmother about his early work schedule last night, she said she could fend for herself and opted to sleep in. So instead of his cooked breakfast, he grabbed two ham and cheese breakfast burritos from the freezer, popped them in the microwave while the coffee perked. Ten minutes later, he was headed down the highway to the first actual construction of one of his engineering plans since leaving the service. The level of excitement surprised him. It wasn't like he was an amateur at this game but putting a plan down on paper then watching it erected from the ground up meant there might be life after the military. That maybe he had found a new purpose in life.

Pulling up to the barn, he noticed a white sheet of paper attached to the door with a nail. He rescued the missive before the wind could blow it away.

Jeremy

Off to the lumber yard to collect the materials for our project. Back as soon as possible. Leave the shovel in the wheelbarrow. You will need all your energy for the construction project.

Grant

The veteran sat down on the sawhorses then leaned against the barn to review the plans in his mind. It had been almost a year since he had put forth any effort to visualize work of that nature. It felt good. Satisfied that he had the design details memorized, Jeremy braced his boots in the loose gravel, pulled his hat over his eyes then crossed his arms over his chest to take a quick nap. It would be a long day.

10

The sounds of a motor gearing down woke the hired hand. Shoving the hat back on his head, he rose to his feet to await the arrival of the flatbed truck Grant used to haul supplies. He was surprised at the amount of rough cut lumber stacked up against the sideboards.

"Did our project grow overnight?"

"They had a two-for-one sale." Grant grinned at the question. "I thought I might as well get enough for two lean-tos, just in case the original building was a success."

"Okay. Where to now?"

"Open the loading gate. I'll drive to the building site after I collect my tool box and posthole digger. Might as well take some hay bales, feed, and water, too. Save us a trip back."

Jeremy did as Grant instructed, secured the lock on the gate afterwards then hopped into the passenger seat. "Now the fun begins."

"If you consider this building project to be *fun*, I seriously wonder about your mind."

"Compared to the last barn duty, this will be a big improvement, boss."

The drive through the pasture wasn't a smooth one as Grant tried to traverse the pot holes left by a previous thunderstorm. Some which were teeth rattling drops similar to a speed bump on a city street. The truck lurched up and out one last time as the fence row appeared. The rancher slowed then reversed to back the truck next to the fence to make it easier to unload.

"Let's lay out the support posts so we have an idea of the corners," Jeremy suggested.

"Okay."

Grant hoisted a rough cut post onto a shoulder and strolled to the far corner while his hired hand placed a similar post in a direct line with the first one.

"I think we will need two posts side by side in the center for structure strength."

Nodding his head in agreement, the Army engineer stepped off the distance and laid the posts next to each other.

"I'll dig while you get the cement ready to pour around them."

"Sure."

Jeremy unloaded the round mixer container, added water to the bag of Set-Quik powder and stirred slowly to make sure no air pockets would weaken the bonding affect. As soon as the post was positioned into the hole, he tipped the container and let the putty colored mixture slowly settle around the post. Then he placed a hand level against the post and adjusted the angle until the bubble was in the center. After waiting five minutes to let the cement harden a little bit, Grant shoveled the dirt from the hole on top, tapped it down hard to make sure the post would remain upright. Again the level was used to see if the post was still plumb.

For the next two hours, this dig, position, and pour process was repeated for all the posts. Soon it was time to attach the wide boards to the three sides and half of the front side before they could staple the plastic sheeting on the rest of the front. Because the back of the lean-to was snug against the fencerow, they attached the boards on that side from the inside. When the last nail was hammered in the last board, Grant paused.

"Let's take a thirty minute lunch break. I picked up some bread, ham, cheese, and all the fixings from the Centerville market before I left town."

"Sounds good to me. Manual labor always gives me a big appetite."

The two men sat on the bed of the truck and savored Grant's version of the Piled High sandwiches with a variety of ingredients, which included everything the deli section had to offer.

"Never had quite this same combination of food stuffs but these are right tasty," Jeremy told him as he stacked the second one.

"My kid sister invented these when she took over the meal planning after Mom died. Kristy said there was bound to be something for everybody to like between the slices of bread."

"How old was she?"

"Ten. Her cooking definitely improved over the years. Trial by error many times but I never complained," Grant said. "I was too afraid she would start throwing things from the kitchen. Sharp things."

"I get the impression she might have a short fuse, if provoked."

"Oh I provoked plenty but she took most of the jibes in stride until Dad died then we both called a truce to have a united force to survive."

"Sounds like you are close to each other."

"As close as a little sister will let a bossy older brother get."

"I missed that bond being an only child."

"There are pros and cons. I tried to protect her long after she was capable of doing it herself."

"I understand the urge to protect. Unfortunately, I haven't found a special woman who will let me."

"Not even a horse trainer?"

"Possibilities could prove interesting." The light in the veteran's eyes was definitely amorous.

"Well my lady love has two fathers who keep me on the straight and narrow. Pete has appointed himself the Bartlett sisters' stand-in."

"I have noticed that already. I don't plan an offensive attack anytime soon."

"With that thought in mind, we better get back to our project if we want to finish before dark-thirty."

The building progressed swiftly as they worked in tandem. The architect and engineer were a good combination. No need to explain what came next. The galvanized tin panels were connected to the corresponding boards with an industrial size staple gun. The slight pitch from front to back of the lean-to would let rain water drain better and prevent cave-in when the winter snowstorms dumped large amounts on top.

"Are these 2X4's left over from the roof for bracing the posts to the long boards?"

"Exactly," Grant replied. "The miter saw and box are in the backseat of the truck."

Using the forty-five degree angle slot, the rancher quickly trimmed the top and bottom edges of the braces, two for each post. Jeremy bored starter holes in the ends of each brace for Grant to attach them with minimum force from the drill bit. Next came the solid plastic sheeting for the front door section. The men fashioned foot-wide cuts to allow the steers to push through to the interior where feed, water, and straw were waiting.

Both men stood back ten feet or so to survey their structure.

"This just might be the best idea I've ever seen."

"Let's hope the herd agrees with you," Jeremy told him.

"I'll round a few head up and push them in this direction.

The smell of the feed troughs should help them walk toward the back wall."

"Okay. I'll wait here and lead the first one inside."

The hired hand didn't have long to wait as a dozen or so steers ambled into sight. He held the plastic sheeting strip aside to let them see what waited for them. Hunger overrode the appearance of the odd shelter for the first cow and a few more followed him like sheep. An odd simile when you thought about it. Grant slapped the rumps of the last few animals when they hesitated.

"Now we let them figure out that it is warmer inside this little building."

"Only time will tell if this idea of mine is a brilliant brainstorm or a big dud," Jeremy said.

Grant nodded in agreement as he began to load the construction equipment back into the bed of the truck while his partner in crime picked up the bits of wood and plastic to leave the area just as they found it. As they bounded back across the pasture, the men remained quiet for the ride back to the ranch house. Conversation after a long day's work wasn't needed.

Arriving back at the gate, Jeremy unlatched the lock and watched as Grant drove through to park the truck beside the barn. "See you tomorrow afternoon," the rancher told his hired hand.

"Goodnight, boss."

Wearily Jeremy climbed into the front seat of his Jeep with much awareness of his aching muscles. It was going to take the whole box of Epsom salt tonight.

11

Jeremy awakened the next morning with an odd feeling of excitement. He lay there with his arms folded under his head and tried to figure out the reason. Was it yesterday's building success or the anticipated riding lesson with the fair Nancy Bartlett? Since wood and plastic sheeting couldn't compare to a flesh and blood woman, the vet had to admit it was the latter option. He smiled at this internal revelation, shucked his boxers, grabbed his robe, and went to take a shower. After a final scrub to his back and shoulders with the long handled bath brush, he rinsed the soap off and wrapped a towel around his waist to finish the morning ablutions. The veteran applied shaving cream to his checks and glided the razor over his chin carefully. No nicks or cuts today. Removing the last bit of shaving cream with a steaming hot washcloth, he paused to look at the items arranged on the countertop.

"Cologne or soothing cream? Which will it be?"

Finally, Jeremy chose the logical over the hopeful. The fresh scent of the skin calming cream would be better than the sting of aftershave lotion. His riding instructor was a practical woman with few, if any, femme fatale tendencies. Nancy was a rare woman who didn't feel the need to apply cosmetics to enhance her natural beauty. A fact that only made him more interested in her. In his experience, it was a bit scary to see a woman's face the morning after when all the artifice was removed. Most times, they didn't resemble the woman of the night before. Jekyll and Hyde dates were always a shock to the system. A chuckle sounded at this gruesome comparison.

The riding student arrived at White's Academy at his appointed time to undertake the next step in his equine instruction to find Ms. Bartlett lazing on the bench just inside the barn door.

Tethered to a stall was an unsaddled mount, Number 3.

"Good morning, Jeremy."

"Good morning, Nancy," he replied with a nod at the horse. "Aren't we practicing today?"

"Yes, but I want you to do the tacking yourself. At the Double L, Grant might not be around to help you with that task."

"Valid point. Self-sufficiency is the goal of these lessons, after all."

The veteran went through the steps of blanket, saddle, and bridle until the horse stood ready for riding.

"I think I remembered your instructions."

"All except one," his instructor answered as she approached the horse. "You didn't reward him for standing so patiently while you put his work clothes on."

Nancy took a sugar cube from her jacket pocket and held it in her palm. Number 3 lipped the sweet treat delicately without doing injury to the fingers.

"Now he's ready for you to ride him. We're taking the riding trail this morning."

"All ten miles?"

"Yes. I think you're ready. Mount up, cowboy."

Jeremy swung up into the saddle then eyed his instructor.

"Technically, I'm not a cowboy."

"Would you prefer tenderfoot?"

"What exactly is a tenderfoot?" he asked.

"A rider who doesn't know one end of a horse from the other."

"I'm not quite that dumb but I guess it is an apt name."

They started off at a slow walk then trot until they were three-quarters of the way back on the trail.

"I think it is time to test your skills at a full gallop."

With this statement, the riding instructor kicked her mount into a faster pace. Soon all Jeremy could see was the tail and flying hooves of the roan.

"Wait a minute. It's not fair for an expert to get a head start," her student called out.

He shook his head then followed her lead. Holding onto the reins tightly, he crouched over the neck of Number 3 to get the least amount of wind resistance. The trainee was almost to the barn gate when he drew alongside Nancy's racing horse. With a swipe of one hand, he flipped her hat off then laughed at her indignant express as she slowed her horse to retrieve her Stetson.

He was waiting by the gate for her to catch up. Jeremy laughed at the fire in the instructor's eyes at this turn of events.

A big grin spread over his face. "Never challenge an Army man, Ms. Bartlett."

Nancy couldn't resist that infectious smile as she grinned back. "I'll remember that for the future. But beware of payback."

The twinkle in his eyes only made her more determined to best him in some way. "Now we get to rub the horses down and put them back in their stalls."

They talked about the upcoming holiday season while they groomed the mounts. Slapping Number 3 on the rump, Jeremy waited until the animal walked into the stall to latch the bottom half of the Dutch door.

"Well, I guess I better get back to the Double L. My shovel awaits."

Nancy strolled beside the veteran as he ambled toward his Jeep. Just as he opened the driver's door, Betsy came out of the house.

"Good morning, Mr. Taylor."

"Why so formal?"

"Well Grant called to invite me to inspect your excellent shelter building. The man credited you with the inventive idea. Therefore, I stand in awe of your brilliance."

"It was nothing that special. A few boards and nails." Jeremy could feel warmth flood his face at her effusive compliment. "I just improvised from past experiences in the desert."

"Well I for one cannot wait to see it. Do you want to tag along Nancy?"

The riding instructor glanced at the flushed cheeks of her student. Maybe payback was coming sooner than she expected.

"I would love to. I think I will ride with Jeremy to find out a little bit more about this talent of his."

The man gave her a look through squinted eyes in suspicion of her docile behavior but went around to the passenger door. "Your carriage, my lady."

Betsy shook her head. Something interesting was happening between those two. She just wasn't sure what as she followed in her own vehicle. She parked beside the house and walked the rest of the way to the cattle barn expecting to see Grant's work truck inside the pasture. Instead, the rancher was sitting on the tractor with a trailer loaded with hay bales, water and feed behind it.

"Is this supposed to be our ride, Lord?"

"Indeed it is. I try not to waste time or resources. One trip to do chores as we tour our guests is more efficient."

"Okay, ladies. Time to climb aboard."

Betsy opted to ride on the tractor fender to be close

to Grant while the riding instructor stepped on the trailer bed then fashioned a chair of several bales of hay. Jeremy retrieved his rubber boots and gloves before he joined his own personal Nemesis among the hay bales.

"Forward hoy, boss."

Even though the tractor was operating in a low gear, the journey was a rough jostling for the passengers.

"I'd better hold on to you, cowboy, so you don't land in the muck," Nancy told him as she held out one hand.

Never one to ignore an invitation, Jeremy plopped down on the hay bale next to Nancy and promptly encircled her shoulders with his arm then whispered in her ear.

"Have no fear, I will protect you."

"This isn't my first hayride, Mr. Taylor."

Since there wasn't much he could say without jeopardizing the situation, the veteran chose to ride in silence with the warm feeling of their bodies huddled close to each other. The bump and sway of the trailer lulled him to sleep. His eyes popped open when the brakes slowed them to a halt. He opened his eyes to find another pair of peepers in direct line with his, eyes that were aglow with amusement.

"Some girls would consider it an insult if a man went to sleep while cuddling."

"And you're not that girl?"

"No. I understand that happens a lot with older men."

Before he could reply to this sassy remark, the woman stepped off the trailer to join Grant and Betsy in front of the structure that looked like a giant hothouse.

"What exactly is the function of this building?" Betsy asked.

"This is Jeremy's idea to keep the cattle that won't come to the barn out of the weather," Grant explained as he pulled the plastic strips open. "Welcome to Taylor Inn."

"I can't take all the credit for this idea. You tweaked it

a bit so you deserve the honor since it is on your land," the hired hand asserted.

"Why don't you call it Lord Taylor Inn?" Betsy suggested.

Grant nodded his head. "I like it. It was collaboration, after all."

The group entered the shelter to find half-a-dozen cattle curled up on the hay strewn ground and another three grazing at the feed troughs.

"It seems to be working, Grant."

"Yes, it does. Now we get to build more 'inns' in the other pastures."

Shaking his head, Jeremy arched his back. "I can feel the muscles protesting already."

"No worries. I have plenty of liniment at the Academy," Nancy told him with a grin.

"Liniment?" Betsy asked innocently.

"Yes. You would be surprised at the medicinal purposes of horse liniment on humans."

Grant looked from his hired hand to the riding instructor then back at Betsy who shrugged her shoulders as if to say, "You're guess is as good as mine".

"Well, we better restock the troughs so we can get the womenfolk back to their own work."

The unloading went quickly. Feed and water troughs were filled to capacity by the men while Betsy and Nancy scattered the opened hay bales in another corner of the shelter.

Grant gave the shelter a quick glance to make sure they had prepped the area completely. "Okay. That should do it. Let's go home."

12

Betsy rested a hand on Grant's shoulder as the tractor and trailer bounced over the rough ground of the pasture. She surveyed the area with the eye of a prospective wife. Cattle grazing on the tufts of grass that dotted the pasture; cattle that would provide meat for the market and money in the ranch ledger. All in all, it was a prosperous business which might result in a June wedding announcement. She wondered if the man was as anxious for that change in her status as she was.

"My college advisor said if I carried twelve credits next semester I could graduate in June."

"That sounds very encouraging." Grant didn't bat an eye at this sudden change in topic from cattle shelters to education. He was getting used to the scattered thinking process of his lady friend that usually meant something else was on her mind.

"I agree. I am ready to get on with the rest of my life."

This comment made the rancher glance at the young woman. The sparkle in his eyes made her sigh with pleasure.

"Would you have any suggestions for that time frame, Mr. Lord?"

"Definitely. I think we need to discuss that topic over dinner Saturday night. Are you free?"

"I am. You can pick me up at seven o'clock." Betsy threaded her fingers through the curls that brushed his coat collar. "I will put you on my calendar."

"You do that, girl."

The rancher let the upcoming dinner conversation run through his mind as he approached the gate into the barnyard. He glanced back at his hired hand to let Jeremy know to open the gate. Once the tractor was parked under the eave next to the barn, Grant offered a hand to Betsy to assist her as she hopped down to the ground.

"That was a most interesting interlude but Nancy and I need to get back to the Academy. A woman's work is never done."

The two men exchanged skeptical looks at this comment.

"Oh, yeah. I'm sure it is backbreaking duty to shuffle papers and ride horses," Jeremy said.

"Don't get uppity, cowboy," Nancy told him. "A barn full of horse tack that needs to be inspected will take several days."

"And the arrangement of those papers into appropriate files can be dangerous if you get a paper cut," the Academy manager solemnly assured them.

Grant tried but failed to keep a wide grin off his face at the confused look in the eyes of the veteran. Female sass must be an odd encounter for someone who dealt with fellow soldiers.

"I'd give up if I was you. You won't win this debate," Grant advised.

"Does that advice come from your vast experience with women, boss?"

"No, son. Just a feisty little sister."

Betsy shook her head at this inane exchange.

"Come on, Nancy. If we stay much longer, we will need to borrow Jeremy's rubber boots."

Grant watched as Betsy rolled down the window of her car to blow him a kiss. "Don't be late Saturday, Grant."

"Yes, ma'am."

Jeremy paused as he helped the rancher unload the trailer.

"It seems this county has an abundance of feisty women. Tell me something, boss. Does feisty translate into passionate?"

"It does, if you are lucky enough to capture the attention of said females." Grant gave his hired hand an inquiring look. "How are your horseback riding lessons going?"

"Good. I can saddle a horse from the hide up now. I should be fairly proficient in a day or two."

"In that case, you can graduate from cleaning stalls to riding fence next week. We need to scout out our next building site."

As Jeremy drove to the Academy the next day, he pondered the attraction he felt for his instructor. Nancy never tried to initiate any kind of romantic situation so he wasn't sure if the attraction was mutual. She had not spurned his overture during the ride yesterday to the Lord Taylor Inn but she might have just been tolerating the closeness due to his injuries. He closed his eyes a second while his brain contemplated that very demoralizing assessment. The veteran knew it was illogical to think that a woman could ignore the scarring on the outside to look at the heart and soul of the man inside. Jeremy reached this conclusion and the road to the stable at the same time. He turned down the paved driveway that accessed the graveled path that lead to his personal Circe.

The instructor silently observed her riding student as he put the halter on his mount then led him out of his stable to complete the tacking process. He was an excellent student. No pausing to think about the next step. Her work was almost done. This thought made a frown appear. It was unfair to make him take more lessons when Jeremy was at this stage of learning. Plus, she needed to get back to her normal routine of exercising the horses. Her student put his foot in the stirrup and vaulted into the saddle like he had done it all his life.

"Ta da! How's that for cowboy expertise? I'm officially a cowboy."

"I agree. You are well trained. Good enough to stop the riding lessons."

"Are you sure? I might have a relapse of equine ignorance," Jeremy said with a grin.

"I'm sure. Only daily practice on your own will make you a better rider," Nancy replied as she looked at him.

Being out in the fresh air and sunshine had put a lot more natural color into his cheeks. When he first started the lessons, his skin had a slightly pale tinge common to people who spent extended amount of time in a hospital. Now his face was tanned a deep brown that made him way too handsome for this cowgirl to ignore.

"In that case, let's take one last trip around the trail."

Not trusting her voice, the riding instructor nodded her head and pointed her horse toward the back of the barn.

The couple rode in companionable silence to let their minds follow the inevitable path that the conclusion of the ride would bring. Arriving back at the barn, they dismounted and rubbed down each horse before putting them back in their stalls. Glancing up, Nancy noticed an odd look on the man's face.

"Is something wrong, Jeremy?"

"No. I was just wondering if you would have dinner with me. I'd like to thank you for your efforts in training a tenderfoot to be a cowboy."

"I'd love to have dinner with you. When?"

"Saturday night at the steak place? Seven o'clock."

"I'll see you then."

Nodding his head in agreement, the veteran turned cowboy walked to his Jeep, climbed behind the wheel, and waved goodbye to the woman who watched the vehicle as he drove away.

*   *   *

Jeremy stood in front of his closet and pondered what to wear on his first official date in over two years. Finally, he settled on khaki slacks, navy jacket with a pullover shirt, which would not require a tie. He didn't want to get too stylist but did want his companion to feel he had made some kind of effort to spruce up. One last check of his face for errant whiskers and he made his way into the living room for his grandmother's inspection. She had gotten so excited that he was venturing out in public that she insisted on making sure he passed muster. He guessed that most grandmothers never thought a little boy grew into a grown man. He almost expected her to smooth the slight cowlick on one side of his head with dampened fingers or check his hands for smudges of dirt.

"Well, what do you think?"

Laura Ann did a slow circle around her grandson. Blinking a tear from her eye, she nodded her head in approval as she patted his cheek. "You look very handsome."

"I think you might be a little prejudiced," the veteran replied as he bent to kiss her cheek. "I won't be too late."

Jeremy checked his wristwatch as he neared the highway turn toward Centerville. There was still fifteen minutes till the hour so he slowed the truck to a crawl. No need to appear too eager.

As he turned down the Academy drive, it dawned on him that he didn't know where to pick up his date. The barn didn't seem likely and there weren't any lights on in the bunkhouse.

Since Pete had appointed himself as surrogate father, I'll stop at the main house.

The welcoming committee that awaited him would have daunted most men. But bombs and IED's had made him of sterner stuff. Still he took a deep breath then walked the short distance to the patio. Four pairs of eyes followed his approach with mixed reactions but his eyes took in the feminine attire of his date. Nancy wore a black skirt and red silk blouse. The vibrant color brought out the flecks of gold in her eyes.

In turn the women's eyes gleamed in appreciation of his evening apparel while the lone male stepped forward with a crease between his eyebrows.

"What's the plan for the evening, son?"

"For heaven's sakes, Pete," Nancy admonished with a shake of her head. "We're only going for dinner at the steakhouse."

"Sorry. Fatherly concern seems to come natural to me. Have a good time."

"Not to worry, sir. With Grandmother's health, my curfew is probably earlier than Nancy's."

Jeremy offered his arm to his riding instructor who accepted the walking aid with a slight dip of her head at this gallant gesture.

The White family waved goodbye to the departing vehicle. Betsy linked her arm with Pete's.

"You heard the man. He will get her home safe and sound."

13

Jeremy and Nancy kept the conversation to trivial things like weather, the next group of Academy students, and his new foray into cattle wrangling. Parking near the front door of the restaurant, the couple walked to the twin doors of the steakhouse. With his hand on the door handle, the veteran took a deep breath and prepared to meet the sympathetic looks from the other diners. It was a natural reaction to his injured face but it still made him uncomfortable. A little of his dismay must have shown in his eyes because his date tucked her hand in his and grinned at his look of surprise.

"No need to worry, soldier. I got your back."

This vow from a wisp of a girl to protect someone who had at least fifty pounds on her slender frame erased the concern from his face. He lifted her hand to place a soft kiss on her wrist.

"Then into the breach we go, sweetheart."

With this comment, the couple laughed as they headed to the hostess stand. Luckily, it was an older woman who had better manners than to react to the scarred face.

"Table for two."

"This way, please."

Following the woman, Jeremy kept a hand on the small of Nancy's back, which allowed him to absorb the warmth of her body through the thin material of her blouse. That was all the physical touching he allowed himself on a first date but his mind went a lot farther. When they reached the linen covered table, he pulled out her chair in his best imitation of a suave Casanova.

"Thank you."

The smile that accompanied this polite phrase made his heart jump a bit, which occurred more often than he cared to admit when he was around Nancy. Bending down he bussed the smooth satin softness of her cheek and whispered just for her ears.

"Did anyone ever tell you that you're beautiful inside and out?'

"Only in my wildest fantasies." The brazen boldness of her reply made her heart pound and her date's eyes gleam.

Ignoring the images this created in his mind, Jeremy took his seat across from her and glanced at the menu the waiter handed to him.

"This place serves a little bit of everything. What are you hungry for?"

Nancy smiled slightly at him and pretended to consider the menu options. She took a deep breath to slow down her pulse to its normal pace.

"I think we should contribute to the local economy and order steak," Jeremy said.

"Sounds good. Make mine medium rare," his date answered. "Since this is a celebration of sorts, I suggest we toast the completion of your training with a cocktail."

"My meds don't mix with alcohol but order whatever you want."

When the waiter returned, the veteran handed him the menu. "Two steaks, medium rare, with loaded baked potatoes and wedge salads."

"And your drinks?"

"We'll take two Perrier's with a twist of lime," Nancy replied. "Add a slice of chocolate cake and two forks."

A chuckle from across the table made the riding instructor blush slightly as she offered an explanation.

"I have a sweet tooth and expect you to save me from myself. I can't afford all those extra calories. They go to my hips."

Jeremy resisted the urge to tell her that her hips looked fine to him. This would reveal to the woman that he watched those same hips whenever she walked in front of him.

After they were served the sparkling water, the couple clinked glasses in mock toast to each other and turned the conversation to safer topics.

"Did your cattle shelter get the results you hoped for?"

"It did. Not completely full but enough to be encouraged. Grant wants to put a few more in the back pastures."

"Sounds like you will be busy with building projects."

"Don't forget mucking stalls."

Soon their steak orders were placed on the table. With gentle probing, Nancy got her date to talk about Grant's plan to patent the shelter plan.

"As soon as the patent is approved, we are going to advertise in the trade magazines to see if other ranchers want to utilize our method of weather protection."

"A website would be a good way to get the message out to the public. Also, provide a site where they can place orders," Nancy told him.

"Probably. Maybe Grant can figure out how to get one set up."

"If not, I'm sure Betsy would be happy to help."

"Again, that would be Grant's department. Can't have my new partner thinking I'm making a move on his girl."

"Since the man is besotted, he could turn violent toward poachers."

"That is the way a man should behave toward the woman he loves." The warm glance he gave her made her lower her eyes.

The object of their conversation entered the restaurant with his girlfriend. Jeremy lifted the last bite of cake to his lips and motioned them over.

"Evening," Grant said. "Didn't realize the whole crew from the Double L was eating here tonight."

"I always try to follow the boss's lead. We even ordered steak to help keep the ledger in the black."

"I appreciate that. If you will excuse us, I think our table is ready."

"We were almost ready to pay the check. Nancy's curfew is looming large," Jeremy grinned. "I fully expect Papa Pete to be sitting on the front porch, shotgun in hand."

Betsy shook her head at this sage comment. "The man can't help it. As soon as he learned of my existence, Pop's protective gene switched into overdrive for all females within his immediate vicinity."

"I expect Grant will have a similar reaction twenty years down the road."

"Damned straight! No Lothario will have a chance to invade the property."

"Good lord. The BS is getting a little deep," Betsy admonished him. "Come along, Grant. I'm getting hungry."

Jeremy and Nancy watched as the rancher tucked Betsy up close to his side and headed to the other side of the dining room.

"They are the perfect couple, aren't they?" Nancy mused.

"Yes. He is a lucky man to have found a special woman to walk beside him."

Jeremy called the waiter over and didn't see the speculative look on his date's face. The look of a woman with a plan.

"Check please."

Within a few minutes, the check was paid, tip money placed discreetly under the salt shaker for the busboy, and the couple headed out to Jeremy's Jeep.

The drive back to the riding academy was filled with companionable silence as they listened to the instrumental CD playing an assortment of Broadway show tunes. The man and woman didn't feel the need to disturb the moment. As the automated sign at the academy driveway entrance flashed on, Nancy glanced over at Jeremy.

"Thank you for dinner. I had a lovely time."

"You're welcome," he replied as he turned down the driveway.

He stopped the Jeep next to the patio so their arrival would be seen by Nancy's watchdog boss. Going around to the passenger door, Jeremy offered a hand to help her to the ground. As soon as her feet touched the gravel, the man tugged her closer. With the other hand, the veteran lifted her chin then placed a soft kiss on her lips.

"Goodnight."

"Goodnight, Jeremy."

Nancy watched as he reversed the vehicle and prepared to leave. Leaning out the window, he called to her. "I'll phone you sometime next week."

Waving from the patio, Nancy sighed deeply and headed to the bunk house.

14

The patent lawyer was busy taking notes as he talked to the men sitting in front of his desk. He stopped writing to examine the sketch on his desktop, which included the suggested building materials.

"So this is a diagram of an easy-construct shelter for cattle?"

"Basically, for any type of ranch animal," Grant answered.

"That wander to the far corners of a large property," Jeremy added.

"What do you want to name this plan?"

"Lord Taylor In with only one 'n'," the rancher replied.

"Okay. I think I have enough pertinent information to work up a mock application. I'll send it to your email in a day or two."

"Thanks, Matt."

Leaving the lawyer's office, the newly formed partnership members paused. "I suggest we have lunch in town before we get down to the serious job of choosing another shelter site."

"I could eat," Jeremy said with a grin. "My appetite seems to have returned two-fold since I started working on the Double L."

"Manual labor and fresh air tends to do that."

"Did you say *fresh* air? Not sure the cattle barn qualifies."

"Point taken," Grant said as he pulled into the parking

lot of a local diner. "I say we load up on double-decker hamburgers and fries."

"As long as they aren't tofu, I'm game."

The men placed their orders and sat sipping their colas while they waited. Since neither one was much of a talker, they just looked around at the regular diners who frequented the eatery. Most of them knew Grant by sight and raised a hand in greeting. Soon the waitress brought the orders. Instead of going back to the kitchen, the woman stayed to chat.

"Here you are, Grant. Haven't seen you around town lately."

"Been busy with the ranch."

"Who's your friend?" The woman gave the other man a quick head to toe glance.

"This is my new ranch hand, Jeremy Taylor. Jeremy this is Sherry Lawson, an old classmate."

"Good to meet you, Sherry."

"And you, Jeremy. You must be new in Centerville. I don't recall seeing you before."

"I recently moved here."

Grant sat back to observe this exchange with a slight smile on his face as he added catsup to his plate. Sherry had been three grades ahead of him when he was in junior high but he remembered that she was a notorious flirt so this should be entertaining.

"Do you dance, Jeremy?"

"Some." His hesitate reply didn't daunt the waitress's interest.

"There is a dance this weekend. You should come by and meet some of my friends."

"I'll ask the girlfriend if she wants to come."

The crestfallen expression on the waitress's face almost made Grant choke on a French fry. He hastily changed his chuckle into a fake cough as he tried to keep his amusement under control.

"Okay. You guys enjoy your food."

Jeremy glared at his tablemate until the woman was out of earshot.

"You could have warned me about the aggressive hunting habits of the women in town."

"Sherry is exceptionally good at that sport and usually takes no prisoners. Although, she might employ handcuffs these days." This remark made his hired hand blush. "Who is this girlfriend you spoke of?"

"No one really. I said the first thing that popped into my head. It seemed a polite way to discourage her advances," Jeremy told him.

"It just might do the trick. But if you decide to attend the dance, you better bring a date or you will have to contend with half-a-dozen females just like Sherry."

"Thanks for the advice."

The men finished their meal without further incidents with the waitress. On the way home, Grant's stop at the hardware store puzzled the veteran.

"Do we need more fencing?"

"No. I want to see if they have any leather chaps in stock."

"Round 'em up and move 'em out clothing?"

"Exactly. You strap them over your jeans. They will save your legs from getting scratched up by the scrub along the fence rows."

"Thanks. My body has enough scars already. Don't need more." After a minute, Jeremy asked another question. "What about the horse's legs? Do they make shields for them?"

"They do but it will take several days to have some shipped in," Grant admitted. "Until then, we can always invent something. Maybe Kris has an idea that would work short term."

Jeremy leaned against the corner of a display counter to observe the one-sided conversation as his boss talked to his sister, a board certified veterinarian who specialized in large animals.

"Had a wild idea, sis. Do you know of anything that I could use to cover the horse's legs to prevent scratches from brambles? I've ordered some regular leg boots but they won't be in for a couple of weeks."

Grant was nodding his head as her suggestions. Hanging up the phone, he paid for the chaps then drove to a sporting goods store. Jeremy wandered alongside his boss until they reached the football accessories department.

"What are we looking for now?"

"Kris suggested that we look for skin protectors like those stretchy compression sleeves that ballplayers wear to prevent leg cramps. They'll adjust to the horse's legs but not cut off circulation."

"It is clear to me that the female in your family got most of the brains."

"And looks," Grant added. "She even volunteered to help put them on since it might take more than four hands to slide them on."

"That sounds ominous."

"My thoughts exactly."

Grant quickly found the sleeves in LARGE. He opted for black so they wouldn't look too conspicuous.

"Now all we have to do is put this plan into action."

Kristy Randolph was sitting on the tailgate of her truck swinging her legs to a tune that blared from the vehicle's radio when the Double L crew arrived.

Frowning at the noise, her brother hurried to the vehicle to turn the ignition key off. "Are you trying to start a stampede with that caterwauling?"

"It is a proven fact that music calms the nerves."

"Not at that volume," he told her with a brotherly arch of his eyebrows. "Do you have a plan to make this project easier?"

"Yes. You and Jeremy hold the horse's head and the leg involved while I slip the sleeves on over the hoof."

"I'd feel better if I did the slipping on. Mitch would have my hide if I let you get kicked in the face."

"Since this job will resemble putting on pantyhose, I figured I have a little bit more practice at that than you. Your forte is taking them off."

Knowing his ears were turning a dull red at Kris's comment, Grant could only nod in silent agreement with her assessment as he studiously avoided Jeremy's knowing eyes and twitching lips.

It took some odd maneuvering but this plan was accomplished without incident mostly because Kris crooned soothing words while she pulled the sleeves up the legs of their two horses.

Standing back, the three ranchers surveyed the mounts.

"Maybe not kosher, but serviceable."

"I am officially insulted by the comical sight but if it keeps the legs safe, it will be worth it."

Grant looked at the other two and grinned. "Okay. Let's saddle up and get this fashion show on the trail, but first we need to don our chaps."

"I'll be home if you need medical assistance," Kris told him as she headed to her truck.

"Did she mean the horses or us?"

A shrug was the only reply from his boss.

The afternoon proved uneventful except for a few snags to the sleeves. The bramble thorns caught the fabric but left the skin unmarred.

The trail hands were on the last section of fence when Grant pulled his horse to a halt. Jeremy followed suit and waited for orders.

"Our next construction project should go right here."

The civil engineer turned cowpoke pulled a red kerchief from his pocket, leaned over his horse's ears, and proceeded to tie it to a fence post.

"That will save time when we bring the materials out tomorrow."

The remainder of their ride was a quiet one as both men's minds were filled with the prospect of the work this would entail.

"Our next project should be to design leg wraps for a horse that will be snag proof. That way we don't have to dismount to untangle the horse's legs. The leather ones don't have any stretch to them. They can slip and chafe the skin."

"I'll give that some thought. Maybe a solution will come to me in my sleep," Jeremy told him.

15

The Double L boss opened his front door the next afternoon to discover his dearly beloved standing on the porch. Her face glowed from the smile that made her beautiful eyes sparkle with mischief. And other things of a more intimate nature. Betsy greeted the men with a saucy grin and wink.

"Your IT tech reporting for duty. Nancy thought you could use my help with a website." A snappy salute accompanied this comment as she walked up to the rancher and stretched on tiptoe for a kiss.

Grant welcomed her with so much enthusiasm that a discreet cough sounded from his hired hand.

"Should I go feed the horses?"

Betsy snuggled closer, patted the muscles under the chambray shirt then arched her eyebrows at Jeremy.

"Alas, I do not have time today for hanky panky. Advanced age makes that activity time consuming."

This sally resulted in a slap to her shapely denim covered derriere from the elderly gentleman in question.

"A merry chase, my friend," Jeremy said as he held a hand to his chest in mock admiration.

"You two should start your own stand-up routine," Grant told them but secretly agreed with his wrangler. Life with Betsy would never be boring. "We need to get this website built so the world can see our project plans."

"Is the coffee fresh?"

"Yes, ma'am."

"Then as soon as I get a cup we can get that plan underway."

The trio huddled together in front of the computer monitor for an hour before they finally agreed on the basic design with a photo of a completed lean-to as an order icon.

"It seems a little blah," Betsy told the men. "It needs some pizzazz."

"It is only a wood and plastic sheeting structure on a working ranch. Cattle won't know pizzazz from blah," Grant said.

"But it needs something to catch the customer's attention. Make them take a second look."

"Any ideas, Jeremy?"

"Don't look at me. My previous experience was building things in a war zone desert. Everything is blah there."

"Maybe I can find a photo of an old-fashioned doorman at a hotel entrance," Betsy told them. "Let's move on to the other features of the website. We will need side view photos of the lean-to to give the customers an idea of the finished project. I will put in a picture box and insert the actual views later."

"Okay. What else will we need on this website?"

"Do you have copies of the plans ready for mailing to those who purchase them?"

"No but I can do that tomorrow," Grant said.

"I'll put a link to the order page. I can add a read-only PDF on the website for them to check the plan out."

The men watched as she did this with a minimum of effort.

"Anything else?" the rancher inquired.

"You will need to set-up a joint bank account separate from the ranch account with automatic credit card sale deposits to keep everything kosher with Uncle Sam."

"Absolutely. Don't want to rile that relative," Jeremy replied tongue in cheek. "What balance should we start with?"

"$500.00 each. That will allow for initial cost of checks, mailing expenses, etc."

"Make us a to-do list, darling. We can cross off the items as we get them done."

Both men looked over her shoulder as Betsy jotted down the duties. Jeremy's sense of humor made him chuckle at the last entry. With a mischievous gleam in his eyes, he asked for clarification.

"Does the last item apply to both partners, Grant?"

When the rancher read the item, he raised a warning eyebrow. "Chaste one on the cheek might be allowed."

"Then I will take mine now." The veteran slung one arm around Betsy's shoulder, tipped her over an arm, and pressed his lips to a cheek that was suspiciously pink.

Upright once more, she punched him on the arm in sisterly fashion at his bit of blarney. "It's going to be a fun time watching you guys work together. The BS is getting deep."

Before the men could think of an appropriate reply, the woman continued.

"Now to an important factor. How much do you want to charge for the lean-to plans?"

"It should be fairly inexpensive so the smaller ranches can afford them," Grant said.

"Is seventy-five dollars low enough?" Jeremy asked.

"Sounds okay to me. That will mean a third to each partner and a third to cover expenses."

With a few more adjustments, the website was ready to be made active.

"I'll take the photos tomorrow so I can finish the job and you boys will be ready for business. I can make the additions from my office computer so you 'partners' can get on with real ranch work."

Jeremy pushed back his chair and stretched. "I best be getting home. Tomorrow will be another long day. Goodnight."

Grant was up at his usual time the next morning. After filling a mug with coffee, he went to enjoy the sunrise from the front porch. As the first streaks of orange and yellow filtered into the horizon, his hired hand parked his vehicle and strode up the steps.

"Any more of that wake-up juice?"

"On the stove. Help yourself."

Soon Jeremy returned to the porch, sat down and quietly absorbed the view while he tried to find words to explain the early arrival without sounding like a school boy.

Five minutes passed before Grant gave him an inquiring look. "Something on your mind?"

"Couldn't sleep so I dressed and drove over here hoping you were awake. I'm always antsy when I start something new."

"I get that way too, sometimes, but I have faith that this new venture will be a success. The mundane day to day duties take care of themselves," Grant said. "Have you had breakfast?"

"Peanut butter toast and OJ."

"I don't have many culinary skills but bacon and eggs I can do. You can talk out your concerns while I cook."

Grant added frozen biscuits to a pan, popped it in the oven then heated an iron skillet to cook the rasher of bacon, enough for the Sanders crew who would be up soon. He picked up the coffee pot and turned to his breakfast guest. "I'll share the last cup and put on another pot."

Jeremy nodded in agreement. "What if nobody thinks the lean-to is worth investing in?"

"Then we find better avenues of advertising. Maybe give away a free set of plans to the first five site visitors."

"Good idea. Five won't cut into the profits too much."

Satisfied that the first problem was addressed, the men set down to finish the meal. The other men wandered in to the kitchen as they were about to leave for another day of lean-to construction.

"Coffee and bacon are ready but you will have to fix your eggs yourself," Grant informed Tom.

Sanders nodded his head. "Have fun today guys."

The building duo developed a system of sorts. Grant sunk holes for the corner posts and Jeremy placed them before adding the cement then piled dirt on top to steady them. Soon they had the lean-to framework in place. Bracing 2x4's came next followed by rough cut lumber boards. Jeremy held them in place while Grant drove the long nails into the posts.

"Let's leave the tin roofing and plastic sheet draping until tomorrow," the rancher told the cowhand.

"No argument from me."

Two sweaty and weary cowboys arrived back at the barn satisfied that the second lean-to was almost finished.

"Give me thirty minutes and I'll have Mile-High sandwiches ready."

"What are you putting in the sandwiches today?" Jeremy asked suspiciously.

"Everything in the fridge. Basically, all the leftovers."

"And they'll be good?"

"Absolutely. Same recipe as those we had at the first building site. Afterwards we can drive to Centerville to set up the bank account"

"Sounds like a good plan. I will fill water troughs and join you shortly."

16

At the text ping sounded from his phone early the next morning, Grant checked to see who had sent the message to both Jeremy and his cell numbers. The read-out only had two words. WEBSITE LIVE. He sent an equally short answer. GREAT! THANKS.

Because Sunday was Jeremy's day off, the rancher performed the daily feed and water distribution to the two lean-tos before he returned to the barn to do the same thing for the herd gathered around the corral fence. He puttered around the barn for another hour but soon all the chores were finished. Betsy had advised him to not look at the website until it was live for one full day. The watched pot theory was her reasoning. He didn't even have the Sanders crew to keep him amused. They worked seven days a week trying to finish José's *hacienda* by the scheduled time. Checking his watch he saw that it was only twelve noon. *Now what do I do to fill the hours?* Guess I'll eat something before I work on the lean-to bookkeeping system.

Rummaging in the fridge revealed leftover casserole that Kristy had brought over one afternoon. Scooping out a generous portion on a paper plate, he put it in the microwave to save time. As he ate, Grant reviewed the bookkeeping items needed for the new venture. Tossing the empty plate into the trash, the rancher went to boot up the computer.

Soon he was elbow deep in the accounting software.

Everything about the debits and credits had to be a separate entity from the cattle ranch accounts. A strict accounting was required since it was a fifty-fifty partnership. Satisfied that all the expense columns were listed including one miscellaneous column, Grant saved the changes and shut down the software.

Checking the time again, he discovered that it was late afternoon. He had just enough time to check the water troughs before he had supper. Turning off the water spigot, he headed to the ranch house. Grant was pulling off his rubber boots when his cell phone rang.

"Double L."

"Hello, darling. It is I."

"Exactly who is 'I'. Any number of females qualify for that title."

"In that case, I will eat my picnic supper all by myself," the voice declared.

"Don't do that, Betsy. You know how much I'd like to see you."

"I do know that but I wonder if it is the food or my company you want."

"Since I am a practical man, I will take the fifth." The laugh that came over the wire made his breathing heat up a notch. "But I can take care of both things with lots of gusto."

"I was hoping you would say that. I can be there in an hour."

*   *   *

The next morning was the first full day after the website went live. Grant booted up the computer while Jeremy sat silently beside him, each wondering if this new venture would sink or swim. Grant clicked on the Lord Taylor In website and stared in disbelief. The list of orders was amazing. At least thirty names appeared as the rancher scrolled downward. Certainly more orders than either of the partners expected. They looked at each other, grinned like Cheshire cats before slapping hands in the usual high-five symbol of success.

"I guess I better load the copier with lots of paper."

After putting two reams of copy paper in the printer, Grant hit print and watched as the list crept from the machine. Pages and pages of orders.

"While you do the plan print-outs, I will work on the address labels for the envelopes," Jeremy said.

Each man was so absorbed in their individual tasks that they didn't notice that the morning passed into afternoon. The sudden roiling growl of an empty stomach broke the silence.

"Sounds like it's time for a quick sandwich before we feed the stock."

Flexing his shoulder to ease the strain on his back muscles from sitting so long, Jeremy nodded his agreement.

Hours later, the men walked from the barn to the ranch house bone weary from the manual labor. Despite this physical condition, their long-legged stride had all the markings of the strut of a male peacock surveying his domain. A "God's in His universe, alls right with the world" philosophy.

As they toed off their manure laden boots at the backdoor, the aroma of food assaulted their noses. The homeowner was immediately suspicious since he had not put anything in the crock pot before they left. Grant pushed open the screen door to discover his kitchen had been invaded by two lovely women. Nancy was icing a chocolate cake while Betsy was busy stirring beef stew in a huge cast iron pot on top of the stove. A large loaf of fresh bread graced the kitchen table.

Looking over her shoulder, Betsy flashed a smile at him. "Food should be ready in twenty minutes or so."

Seeing his woman busily fixing a meal for him, made Grant realize how much he loved and needed her to share his life everyday. His heart swelled with emotion as he placed a soft kiss on her cheek.

"Just enough time to shower."

Betsy placed a hand on his chest to hold him away and wrinkled her nose. "It would be much appreciated."

Jeremy had watched this scene with much wonder as he experienced a mixture of feelings toward Nancy but knew their relationship was not as advanced as the other couple. They had only known each other a month. His normal cautious nature of slow, baby steps when it came to a lasting relationship with a woman would not work this time. He realized he needed to speed up the process. It had been a while since he had seriously courted a woman but he needed to stake a claim while Nancy was still available.

He approached her to check out the mixing bowl. A glance revealed that only a smear of icing coated the bottom of the bowl. He removed the spatula from her hand to taste the velvety richness with one swipe of a tongue. "How did you know my favorite cake was chocolate?"

"You helped me eat my dessert when we had our dinner out, remember?"

"I remember a lot of things about that night."

Seeing the sudden blush on her face, it pleased him to know she had paid such close attention to him that evening.

"I guess I better hit the showers, too. Hopefully, Grant didn't use all the hot water."

Thirty minutes later, both men returned to the kitchen with the clean scent of soap instead of the aroma of livestock. The table was set with all the proper settings for a meal; china plates, silverware, and napkins. Something Grant and the construction crew dispensed with whenever they happened to be at the ranch at the same dinner time. The long hours Tom's crew spent working on José's *hacienda* meant they made due with sandwiches and chips washed down with lots of beer.

After filling their plates with seconds, Jeremy complimented the cooks.

"Awesome food. It definitely hits the spot."

"Jeremy's right. We were going to heat up leftovers so this meal is a welcome substitute. And as much as I appreciate the good vittles, I don't remember that we had a date scheduled for tonight."

"No schedule just a spontaneous outpouring of pity for your cooking abilities," Betsy told him. Seeing a disbelieving look from the rancher, she grinned. "Actually, I checked the website at noon and noticed all the orders for the lean-to. We decided to come over to stuff envelopes and came bearing gifts in the form of food."

"A woman who is pretty and considerate is a heady combination for this old cowboy."

"And his much younger protégée," Jeremy added with a wink at Nancy. "Is it time for cake?"

"I don't know where you'll put it but dessert and coffee coming up."

After satisfying everyone's sweet tooth, Betsy assessed the stack of orders then used her office manager skills to organize an assembly line of sorts for efficiency.

"Okay. Grant, you and Jeremy fold the plans and stack them on one end of the table where Nancy will put them in the envelopes to create another stack." Betsy paused to take a sip of coffee. "Then I will apply mailing labels, seal them, and box them up. No need to put stamps on them until we see how much they weight at the post office."

So began the stuffing and labeling. Even with four

workers, it took almost two hours to finish. The proof of their labors was a full box of fat envelopes sitting on the kitchen table.

"I worked up an appetite with all that manual labor. Is there any cake left?" Grant asked.

"Yes. But don't you want to save some for the construction crew?"

"Not really. You snooze you lose is my philosophy."

Shaking her head at his attitude, Betsy went to the kitchen.

Nancy followed. "I'll cut the cake, if you will make another pot of coffee."

"Deal."

The last of the dishes had been washed, dried, and put away when boots sounded on the front porch. The screen door opened to admit the Sanders crew.

From his relaxed seat on the couch, Jeremy gave them a serious look. "Man you work some long hours."

Tom nodded his head in agreement.

"There is plenty of beef stew if you aren't too tired to eat," Betsy announced.

"Sounds good," Sonny told her. "Showers first. Thirty, forty minutes or so."

"That will give Nancy and me time to warm up the food."

Since the loaf of bread was gone, a large pan of biscuits was popped in the oven.

"Grant, you and Jeremy can set the table since you seem to have recovered from the evening's work."

"You know, Jeremy, the woman has a bossy side."

"I did notice that earlier when she was assigning jobs. I fully expected to see her break out a whip."

"Yes." Grant considered that option for a second. "I just might buy her a whip so she can herd the cattle."

Betsy eyed the men before replying. "Whips can be used on more than cattle, or so I've heard."

The construction crew walked up just as this sassy comment was delivered which made the cook's cheeks blush a faint pink. Grant laughed at her obvious embarrassment which elicited arched eyebrows from the woman.

Tom looked from one to the other and decided he must have misunderstood the woman.

"I'm not even going to ask."

"That's okay. Just a bit of joking. The biscuits should be ready in five minutes."

"Since Grant and Jeremy ate all the cake," Nancy declared, "I stirred up a peach cobbler. It should be ready soon, as well."

Vitorio sniffed the air like a bloodhound. "Chocolate?"

"Yes."

"You know you aren't a very hospitable host, Grant."

"Not when it comes to dessert." Looking at Nancy, he posed a question. "Do you mean to tell me I had the ingredients for cobbler in my kitchen cabinets?"

"Yes. I'll jot it down for you. It is such a simple recipe that even a man can prepare it."

"Did the woman just insult our culinary skills, Tom?"

"Sounded like it but if the cobbler tastes as good as it smells, I can forgive her."

The Sanders crew made short work of the stew and biscuits. Hot cobbler and vanilla ice cream rounded out the late supper.

Jorge gathered up the dishes and took them to the kitchen sink.

"I'll wash those," Nancy told him. "You've had a long day."

"Thank you. Is Diane as good a cook as you?"

"Horses are more her bailiwick but she can boil water and order take-out."

Grinning at this quip, he snagged the last biscuit. "Goodnight."

17

The three women gathered around the Academy office computer were there to decide on the perfect invitation to hand out to their Thanksgiving meal guests. While Betsy was busy photo shopping the design, Gwen and Kristy jotted down names of the invitees which included the White family and riding academy staff, the construction crew, Randolph family and José, Grant, Jeremy Taylor and his mother.

"That makes sixteen people on the list," Kristy announced.

"What about the new Ridge cowhand?"

"Bobby Joe Johnson has family in Butte and he told me he'd be headed there for the meal."

Gwen gave her stepdaughter a glance then made a suggestion.

"Would you like to invite Donna and the Sheriff to this shindig, Betsy?"

"That is a lovely thought," Betsy smiled at her step-mother. "And thank you for thinking of them. Mother and Daddy would probably rather spend the day with a rowdy bunch of people rather than eating alone or an impersonal meal at the steak house."

"Well, like it or not Pete and the Sheriff are family now. They will just have to get used to seeing one another at family functions," Gwen told her.

"Agreed. That will make eighteen bodies to gather around the table. Two chairs to spare."

"Last but not least, the menu," Gwen declared.

"Mitch can smoke a turkey and a couple of hams," Kristy offered.

"That takes care of the entrees. Now what kind of side dishes do we want?" Betsy asked.

Chewing on the end of a pen, Kristy contemplated her friends. "I guess we should have three or four vegetables and maybe a salad."

"I can do my chicken and dressing with brown gravy," Gwen told them.

"Why don't we ask the guests to bring their favorite side dish? That way everybody will contribute to the meal. The single guys can do dinner rolls or soft drinks. Maybe even a bottle or two of wine."

"Great idea, Kris. I'll put a BYOSD on the invitation with an asterisk notation to call for details," Betsy said.

The next thing to do was agree on the invite design, print them up, and address the envelopes. This plan was not a difficult one. Within an hour, the invites were ready to give to the guests.

"Hand delivery would be best. That way we know they received them," Gwen said.

Betsy printed out a list of guests with a column for food items.

"I think our labors deserve a glass of wine," Gwen told the party committee.

"I agree," Kristy agreed. "I need something to get the taste of glue off my tongue."

"Let's take our glasses into the den. Relax in front of the fire," Betsy told them.

That is where Peter White found the women as he walked in from the corral. Chatting and laughing, feet on the coffee table, they held up their glasses to toast the master of the house.

"Here's to Pete, the man of the hour."

"What's going on, ladies?" In spite of the comic scene, he tried to sound serious.

"We're celebrating an afternoon of total success, Pop," Betsy informed him.

Pete noticed the empty bottle on the coffee table before he replied. "I thought wine, women, and song were a male prerogative."

"Yes, but we are advanced models of womanhood," Kristy told the old Ridge foreman. "And this one has to go home to the husband. Goodnight, all."

"Goodnight. Kris. Thanks for your help."

"Not at all. I just appreciate you volunteering your banquet size table for the event."

Pete escorted his neighbor to her truck. "Drive safe. Mitch will have my hide if you end up in a ditch because of blurred vision due to alcohol fumes."

"It would take more than a couple of glasses of wine to inebriate me, but thanks for your concern."

Pete watched her drive away with perfect precision before he walked back into the house. His lovely wife and daughter had picked up the glasses and gathered around the kitchen island bar looking at cookbooks.

"What are you in the mood to eat, darling?"

Since he wasn't sure how steady her hand might be with utensils, he smiled. "How about two large pizzas? Nancy and Diane can help us eat them."

"Excellent idea. You shower and I will call in the order for delivery."

Fresh smelling with damp hair that curled around his collar, the man of the house helped himself to a beer from the fridge. He noticed the invitation that was posted on the menu board beside the patio door. Everything looked normal until he got to the bottom of the page.

"What does BYOSD stand for? Doesn't sound edible."

Gwen looked at him in amusement. "BRING YOUR OWN SIDE DISH."

"I still don't get it."

"If each guest brings a dish, it will truly be a community meal."

Finally Pete understood and nodded his head in agreement. "I'm so glad the women in this family are so intelligent. I'll be in the great room. I think there is a football game on the telly. Let me know when the pizza arrives."

His wife and daughter shook their heads at his single-minded pursuit of sports then went back to perusing the cookbooks.

"Better call the Bartlett's. Let them know that dinner is on the way."

Gwen phoned down to the bunk house.

"Pete's cooking dinner tonight."

"Does that mean pizza?"

"Of course," Gwen told them.

Soon Nancy and Diane wandered in to join the ladies at the island.

"What's with the cookbooks?" Nancy asked.

"We are searching for foods to serve at our three-ranch Thanksgiving celebration," Betsy replied. "Your formal invitations are on the counter."

Diane handed one to her sister and opened hers. After reading it, the riding instructor asked the same question as Pete. "BYOSD?"

"We are requesting that each guest bring a side dish to go with the turkey, ham, and traditional dressing with gravy," Betsy told her.

"And for those who don't cook, they can bring rolls or

beverages," Gwen told the young woman whose panicked look was a bit comical. It was well documented that Diane was not inclined to be domesticated.

"Not to worry, baby sister. I can prepare two dishes for our family's contribution."

"Whew! That was a close call."

"Yes, but you really need to learn at least the basics of cooking. Otherwise a husband and children will starve," Nancy admonished her.

"Since I don't anticipate either in the near future, cooking school can wait."

A horn sounded from the driveway to announce the arrival of their dinner.

"Soups on, old man," Gwen declared with a wink at the other ladies.

While the owners and staff of the White Riding Academy munched on the spicy pizza, they discussed the general condition of the horses and equipment which was the riding instructors' task until the school's spring session began in April.

18

José picked up the barn phone on the third ring. "Randolph Ridge."

"Hello. Tom Sanders here."

"Is there a problem with the *hacienda*?"

"No. I thought you might want to do a walk-through to check the progress before we get to the final stages."

"Si. I can be there in fifteen minutes."

The construction crew sat under the overhang of the *hacienda* drinking coffee to await the home owner's arrival. When José rattled up in the Ridge "mule", he skidded to a stop amid a swirl of dust. Tom watched as the new foreman strolled through the arched doorway of the courtyard. The wrought iron gates leaned against the wall, waiting to be hung to proudly proclaim that it was Vargas property. In one corner, neatly stacked bricks were ready to be laid for a wide paved walkway from the gate to the front door, reminiscent of the streets of Old Mexico and the perfect way for visitors to avoid trampling mud into the house.

He glanced around the area then smiled as he saw the tiny poplar tree sapling that was planted inside the stone seat in one corner. It would be many years before it would provide enough shade for an early evening rest after a hard day on the horse ranch. José walked over to examine the tiny tree.

"Not to worry. The tree will grow quickly," Vitorio told

the *hacienda* owner. "I will put bracing lines so it will grow straight and tall."

"Gracias. You have accomplished a great deal in such a short space of time."

"Grant told us to have it ready for you to move in Christmas week," Tom told him. "Something about Santa coming early this year."

"Then I better check out the interior so you can finish on time."

José wandered around the empty rooms trying to imagine them with the usual furniture. In the huge living room, he sat down on the raised stone hearth and stared at the adobe walls. At this moment they were plain, unadorned stucco surfaces that begged to be decorated. He needed to look for a mural painter because he wanted a fiesta scene like the ones he remembered from his childhood when his parents toured the village where they were born.

Tom watched the various emotions chase over the foreman's face with interest. It almost seemed like he was daydreaming of another life in another place and time.

"Close your eyes then tell me what you see."

José gave him a self-conscious smile but did as he suggested. A full blown scene appeared on his eyelids. A smile curved his lips as he spoke.

"A much simpler time during a harvest festival to celebrate the abundant crops that year. Where the village senoritas danced in the square, their full skirts whirled to the sound of castanets. And caballeros in fancy suits adorned with glittering stones. Their outfits are completed by the rowels on their boots that jingle as they keep time to the music and walk on the bricked surface of the street. The men try to catch the eyes of a particular young woman and wait eagerly for the chance to court her."

"Then that is what you should have depicted on the stucco surface."

"I was just wondering if you knew of such an artist who can do the work."

"Not off the top of my head but I can check with the crew," Tom replied.

"Everything looks fine. Go ahead with the final touches," the foreman told him. "I have to get back to the Ridge. I'm checking references on resumes. I need to interview men next week to fill my old job of horse wrangler, whose primary job is looking out for the brood stock."

"Good luck with that."

José climbed aboard the utility vehicle and away he went in another cloud of dust. Bounding over the old trail that led from his property to the Randolph ranch, he waved to the couple who strolled hand in hand toward the cottonwood trees on the edge of the White Riding Academy property. They were so absorbed in each other they didn't even know he was around. It must be nice to be young and in love.

His thoughts returned to the men who were to be interviewed. They had already hired one hand, Bobbie Joe Johnson, who was in charge of keeping the barn clean and riding equipment repaired, but they needed an experienced man to care for the pure bred stallions. Maybe after he found the second hired hand, he might have time to check out the ladies in Centerville. That *hacienda* would be too big, too quiet for one person. It needed noise and happy laughter.

*   *   *

José would have been surprised at the alertness of the man who walked in that field. The veteran knew exactly what was going on in the surrounding area. He had not survived his tour of duty in Afghanistan by ignoring activity around him. He just chose to concentrate on the feel of the hand he clasped lightly in his. When he glanced over at the woman, he caught her sigh of contentment. He wondered if it was the unexpected afternoon off or being in his company that caused the expression. Jeremy hoped in was the latter.

"What's on your mind, Nancy?"

"Just thinking how nice it is to be here and wondering if that wonderful aroma coming from the picnic basket is your mother's famous fried chicken."

So much for his romantic musings, the soldier thought. "Yes, it is. Along with German potato salad, yeast rolls, and a whole lemon icebox pie."

"Wonderful! All this exercise is making me hungry."

"And here I thought it was my scintillating company you craved," Jeremy teased.

"That is a nice bonus because I don't go walking out with just any man."

They had arrived at the tree line and he let those words sink into his heart. "Will this spot do for our luncheon, madam?"

"Yes," Nancy told him. "Let me spread this blanket out before we get down to the serious business of eating."

Jeremy sighed and shook his head at her practical approach to the romantic setting he hoped to create when he suggested this impromptu meal. The woman was nothing if not practical.

Conversation was ignored as they filled plates with food and began to eat. It wasn't until Nancy helped herself to a piece of pie that he began to speak again.

"How go the plans for the next riding school session?'

"Betsy thinks we will have a full house again, which means my job is secure for the next few months."

"I suppose there will be lots of work to get the horses and equipment in tip top shape."

"That is a sure bet. Why do you ask?"

"Thought we might have time for a dinner date in Centerville once in a while before it gets too crazy. If you like?"

Nancy examined her picnic companion's face since his tone was light. A little too light. *I wonder what this man is up to.* Aloud she asked a question in reply to his.

"Is your workload such that you can make these kinds of future plans?"

"I think so. The riding is getting easier. Next I plan on trying my hand at herding the cattle into the branding chutes or maybe even roping a calf. But that is only during the daylight hours. Not after dark when most folks stop working to have dinner."

"I guess we can schedule a meal or two now and then. I'll let you know when I'm free."

Jeremy smiled at her, leaned against the tree trunk then picked up the plate to enjoy the pie and coffee. Maybe even a nap afterward secure in the knowledge that the plan to woo the woman was headed in the right direction.

When his cell rang three days later, Jeremy was surprised to see Nancy's name on the read-out. "What's up, darling?"

"Do you have two left feet?"

"Not the last time I checked. Why?"

"The last Fall Dance is this Saturday night. I thought we might double date with Diane and Jorge."

A frown appeared between his eyebrows. "I didn't think you approved of him."

"I just might have misjudged him. He should at least get a chance to prove me wrong."

"Okay. What time?"

"Seven-thirty. See 'ya."

Nancy hung up the phone then turned to see Pete

standing in the barn doorway with an odd expression on his face.

"Making a date for your sister and Jorge?'

She felt compelled to explain. "Yes. For the dance this weekend. Something for her to remember after he goes back to Arizona."

Pete nodded his head. "Good idea. We may have been too hard on him."

With that sage comment, the Academy owner headed back toward the house. That was when he got another idea. As he entered the house, he dialed a number. The Ridge foreman answered.

"I need a favor, José." Pete explained the proposed dance date. "I think you should go along and make sure the local good ole boys don't give him a bad time."

"You want me to chaperone a grown man?"

"Yes. I don't want the girls to have to referee a fight. You can tell them you are shopping for a housekeeper."

"You're funny, Viejo. Very funny," the foreman replied. "But I'll go."

"Thanks. Knowing the Bartlett girls they'd want to help fight."

*   *   *

José parked his truck beside Jeremy's Jeep and joined them inside just as a group of cowboys approached the two men who were waiting on the Bartlett girls to hang up their coats.

"Do you guys even know how to dance?" The question was laced with an obvious challenge.

With a glance at Jorge and José, the veteran replied tongue in cheek as a crooked smile revealed a dimple in his cheek. "Line."

José gave a cocky grin of his own as he added. "Hat."

Jorge crossed his chest in true Apache style to announce in a deep rumble. "Rain."

The three cowboys nodded to each other as they stood in solidarity as they awaited the verdict from the other men. Fun or fight was their choice.

This calm way of answering made the belligerent men laugh and the tension of the moment was dissolved. Evidently the comical replies set the mood.

Nancy and Diane joined their dates and suggested they join the other people on the dance floor.

"You children go along now. I'm going to check out those ladies at the concession table," José told them.

The two couples were content to hold each other in their arms. They danced in a tight circle with a slow shuffle to every song regardless of the tempo. The occasional comment was in a whispered cadence meant only for the dance partner's ears.

José kept a watch on his friends as he sipped a soda and chatted up a couple of the ladies, who flirted with him. Knowing they must have heard about his inheritance, he decided to see if their interest was him or his money.

When he mentioned that he wasn't looking for a wife but somebody to keep house, the offended looks from the women surprised him. Or was it amusement? The smirk on his face suggested he knew exactly what their reactions would be before he spoke. He didn't intend to give any of the women a chance to misunderstand his intentions. The Ridge foreman didn't have time to avoid pursuits by any determined women. Left to his own devices, José tapped his boot to the music.

19

The following Monday, the foreman reached the barn just as the first hired hand candidate arrived. From the brand new truck he drove as well as the fancy boots he wore, José felt a slight misgiving about his suitability for the job. This young man...the resume listed him as twenty-five... looked too affluent to appreciate the room and board that came with the salary the boss had told him to offer. A brief conversation with the man proved the foreman's assessment to be accurate. Picking up the resume to check for a contact number, he addressed the applicant.

"I have several more men to interview but we will contact you later with our decision."

After the shiny truck drove away, José put a red 'X' on the resume before he turned it facedown on the hay bale that served as his desk. While he waited on the next candidate, the foreman read through the other six, hoping that some bit of information would strike his fancy.

Most of them had the required experience but facts on paper didn't necessarily give a true glimpse of the type of man they were. Only by looking a man in the eye could you get a gut feeling about his honesty. The Randolph Ridge had too many valuable horses to let just anybody take care of them.

"I'll introduce the next few men to the Black. If the

crazed wild snort the stallion offers to any stranger didn't scare a man off, he just might be the one."

When José realized he was talking out loud to himself, he paused to take a deep breath to reset his brain. Anybody hearing him would think he was not completely rational. With the Black plan in mind, José stacked the rest of the resumes in order of age then experience. Mostly because an older man would not be apt to flirt with the missus, something neither he not the boss would tolerate.

As a dusty pick-up truck with a multitude of scratches stopped in front of the barn, José walked out to greet the man whose jeans were clean but frayed in places. It was evident that he didn't waste his money on fashion or the latest high-tech vehicle.

"How do you do? I'm José Vargas, the Ridge foreman."

The applicant smiled slightly and shook the hand he offered. "Hello. George Jones but everybody calls me 'Slim' for obvious reasons."

"With that name I suppose it helps to prevent requests for a song or two."

"Absolutely. Because I can't carry a tune in a bucket, as the saying goes."

"How did you hear about the position?"

"Bobby Joe Johnson mentioned it to his sister who told my Mom who told me," Slim explained with a slightly embarrassed smile.

It was the normal grapevine method of spreading news in cow country.

José grinned in appreciation of the man's amiable personality. "Let me show you the corrals."

The foreman led the way through the barn to the main corral where the resident stud horse roamed. As he knew the horse's habits, it wasn't long before an ebony streak raced to the fence, skidded to a halt, shook his head, and snorted loudly at the men. The applicant didn't flinch at the greeting from the famous stallion.

"Whoa, there boy. Aren't you a beauty?" Slim extended his hand toward the massive head.

After a few seconds, the horse nosed the hand. "Is he looking for a carrot?"

"Mrs. Randolph has spoiled him a little bit. He prefers sugar cubes." José shook his head before he reached into his shirt pocket for the sweet treat and placed it in the palm of one hand. The Black revealed large teeth as he nibbled it daintily with his lips.

"Is he always so calm?"

"No. He's been known to kick down his stall if agitated by some animal scent he thinks has invaded his territory, especially if a mare is in estrus."

"That is a natural defensive mechanism for a breed horse of his caliber."

José studied the man's face for a second or two before he spoke. There was no odd or greedy expression in his eyes "So you know the Black."

"His reputation has spread pretty far in this Western country. I worked a few ranches in the Butte area and the bosses always talked about his blood lines."

"They are impressive. That's why he draws big stud fees."

Again he studied the man. He could not detect any avarice in his eyes. Right then and there, the ranch foreman made an executive decision. He would take a chance on this man who walked beside him.

"Let's get in out of the sun while I give you a few details about the job."

José outlined the perks of the position, which included a small furnished cabin complete with kitchenette nestled in back under the cottonwood trees.

"Of course, the hours can be long ones and backbreaking

at times. Horses are a twenty-four/seven responsibility but you will have evenings off unless there is some emergency. There are only two stipulations. No smoking in the barn. Alcoholic beverages are allowed off the clock, but absolutely no drinking while you're working. What do you think of those conditions?"

"I think they suit me just fine, if you will hire me, Mr. Vargas."

"The job is yours. You can move into the cabin and start tomorrow. We don't stand on ceremony around here, Slim. Call me José."

"Thank you, José. I only have a few things in the back of the truck. I'll unload them now if it's okay with you."

"That's fine. The road that circles around the barn leads to the cabins. Yours is the first of the smaller cabins. Here is the key," José told him. "I'll be at the main house. Come find me when you get unloaded. I'll introduce you to the boss."

José picked up the rest of the resumes and called the other candidates to let them know the position had been filled.

Slim drove around and parked underneath one of the cottonwood trees then unlocked the cabin. The hired hand plopped his Stetson on the side table under the coat rack at the door and looked around at the space. Simple furniture filled the living area along with a forty-eight inch TV with DVD player and a modern stereo for entertainment. In the bedroom, he found a double bed, a chest of drawers. The adjoining room held a small bathtub and shower stall. A look into the kitchen revealed a microwave and stove. The cupboards held a good supply of canned goods and the small refrigerator had sodas, water, and a six pack of beer. Off the kitchen area was a utility room with a stacked washer dryer combo. It would be nice to have a place all to himself. The other ranches he worked on had bunkhouses with noisy bunkmates.

Slim had one suitcase and a duffle full of chaps, gloves, boots, along with all the other items a horse wrangler needed. The new hand placed the suitcase on the thick comforter but decided to wait to unpack. Slim didn't want to keep the big boss waiting too long. He slipped his hat back on and began his walk to the ranch house he had seen on his way to the barn.

As he approached, he recognized the dark haired man he had seen at an auction barn a few years ago with old man Randolph. The young man was a little older now but clearly a direct descendant of James Randolph. The same strong jaw assured him that the man could take care of anybody who dared to trespass. But it was the woman sitting on the swing who made him blink in surprise. Even with her red-gold hair tied in a pony-tail, she was incredibly beautiful.

The three people sitting on the patio watched as the new hired hand strolled toward them. José had filled Mitch Randolph in on the man's credentials and his assessment of his ability to take over the empty wrangler position. When his boots hit the patio bricks, the Ridge owner stood up and greeted him with extended hand. The new wrangler met his eyes directly. No sign of excessive indulgence in either drugs or booze. That was a bonus in his favor for the owner.

"Afternoon. Welcome to Randolph Ridge. I'm Mitch Randolph and this is my wife, Kristy, who takes care of all the paperwork for the ranch. She is also our resident vet."

Slim tipped his hat to the woman with a respectful "Ma'am" before he gripped the hand of his new boss.

The men talked horses for a few minutes but soon José donned his own hat. "Time to show Slim around and explain the daily chores."

"Thanks for the opportunity to work for you, Mr. Randolph."

"You're welcome. We hope you will find it a good place to ply your trade."

With a nod and another tip of his hat, the new wrangler followed the Ridge foreman back toward the barn.

"Your duties will be primarily tending to the blood stock and seeing that they are healthy. If you notice anything out of the ordinary, let Kristy know."

Slim nodded and trailed along with the foreman as he stopped at each stall in the barn to detail the period of gestation which let the big boss know when to expect the foals. At the end of the tour, he knew that this was the most organized horse ranch with which he had ever been associated.

"I'll go get my working clothes and boots on so I can start getting to know the layout of the ranch," Slim told José.

"You can wait until tomorrow if you want to get settled in the house."

"I'm not one to twiddle my thumbs. I'd rather keep busy. I can unpack after the sun goes down."

"Okay. If you have questions, give a holler."

20

The White household was abuzz early in the morning with all the food preparations needed for the Thanksgiving meal. The kitchen traffic looked like a beehive with several queens in full hive mode. Each of the guests who had accepted the invitation was contributing side dishes. The pork loin was ready to pop in the oven and the turkey and hams had been slow cooking since daybreak in the Randolph's smoker that had been trucked over the day before Even the new hired hand, Slim, had furnished several cans of jellied cranberry sauce. While the men gathered in the great room discussing the upcoming football game, the ladies put all the food except the meats on the decorative runner on the massive table.

Soon the smell of the meat wafted into the house and Pete wandered outside to check on the roasting meats. A thermometer inserted into the turkey breast assured him that the bird was ready to take inside and the brown sugar glaze on the hams glistened with a deep caramel color. Gwen removed them from the roasting pan to let it rest a bit before the man of the house carved them up. While it was cooling, Gwen drained the juices from the pan into a big skillet to make the gravy the men liked to pour over everything. Five minutes later, the food was all assembled on the table.

"Chow time, boys."

The clatter of boots on the floor sounded like a herd of

horses as the men picked a seat beside the lady he fancied. Jorge Destchin had managed to commandeer the chair next to Diane Bartlett with Bonita and Vitorio beside him. Soon the guests stood behind the chairs waiting for their host to speak.

"Welcome to our home." Pete looked around at the various nationalities represented by his guests. "We give thanks for all the blessings of family and friends this day."

Vitorio Destchin picked up his glass and lifted it into the air. "We aren't of the Wampanoag tribe who celebrated that first Thanksgiving feast but we are honored to be included in such a loving family event. Salud."

Each guest tapped their glass to the next person like the falling of dominos until the last glass was touched on the way back to Vitorio.

"Let us pray."

"Make it short, Pete, I'm starving," Grant informed him. "The aroma of all this food has piqued my appetite."

"Bless this food and this hungry horde, Lord. Amen."

Amen echoed through the house as chairs were pulled out for the women before the men took a seat.

"Carve the turkey, Pete, while we pass the rest of the food around," Gwen requested of her husband.

The next hour was spent heaping food onto plates and refilling them as long as the food on the platters and bowls lasted. The dining room table conversation centered on cows, horses, and the next session of the riding academy.

"How goes the bookings?"

"Filled to capacity for the spring and part of the summer sessions. The word has spread about the riding school. We've got students coming from all over the country," Pete declared with pride.

"Which will keep the old man out of trouble," Betsy said with a wink at Pete who grinned at his child.

"I've known Peter White all his life," Laura Ann Taylor said. "Not sure that is possible but he has morphed into a good man. Proud to call him a friend."

"Thank you. I've been working hard at it."

"Mercy. We have gotten serious all of a sudden. Where is the dessert?"

Gwen sliced up the cakes and pies while Betsy arranged mugs and one regular one decaf coffee thermos on the island counter. Diane and Nancy loaded the dishwasher to full capacity.

"Dessert and coffee are buffet style. Help yourself. You can take the food into the great room to enjoy while you watch the game," Gwen told them. "Just bring your plates to the sink when you finish."

A round of buffet hopping happened as the men tried to get a portion of each dessert on their plates. Some migrated to the great room while some lounged in the dining room archway. With much moaning and groaning about eating too much, the men left plates on the counter then proceeded to take a nap during halftime.

Soon all the dishes were scraped clean of the remnants of food and stacked on the kitchen counter waiting for the next dishwashing load. The womenfolk helped themselves to dessert and collapsed at the table to enjoy the sweets and put their feet up.

"My feet are sore from all the walking around the kitchen this morning but I think the meal was a complete success," Gwen declared.

"I agree," Kristy replied. "Just think. We get to do this all over again for Christmas dinner."

Deep sighs were the responds from the rest of the women as they lifted forks full of cake and pie into mouths.

"I will need to walk around the riding trail after eating all this food," Nancy told them. "Anybody want to join me?"

Looking up, she encountered the eyes of her former riding student. A slight smile pulled across his face.

"I'd best come with you to protect you from any wandering animals."

After putting on coats, scarves, and gloves to combat the night temperatures, the couple walked out the patio doors headed toward the stables.

"I wonder who is going to protect Jeremy," Diane remarked to the rest of the women.

This comment made the other ladies smile as they considered the outcome of such a walk in the moonlight.

The aforementioned man tucked the gloved hand of his companion into his and matched his stride to hers at they strolled toward the riding trail.

"Don't want to lose you in the darkness."

Nancy smiled at his foolishness. "How are the shelter plan orders coming along?"

"Very well."

"And your riding skills?"

"The horse hasn't thrown me yet."

Nancy sensed that Jeremy was pre-occupied so she let the sound of the wind in the trees take the place of conversation. The artic breeze made their breath a foggy mist as they walked along the well worn path.

The couple halted at the trail turn-around. Breathing in the crisp mountain air, the soldier knew he had to speak his mind or the moment would be gone.

"I've only been back in Centerville for a few months but it feels like home, which surprised me."

"Why is that?" Nancy leaned against the fencing and gazed at the stars. They were so bright you could almost reach up and touch them.

Jeremy kept a close eye on her face as he began his speech.

"I grew up in the city then went off to war where chaos

was the norm. The slow pace of this small town and peaceful atmosphere of ranch life made me content for the first time in my life."

"That's a good thing, isn't it?"

The man placed his hands on her shoulders to turn her toward him. The look in Nancy's eyes gave him the courage to continue.

"The place and work isn't the only thing that made this feeling of belonging. Meeting you has changed my way of thinking about a lot of things. Mostly, the future and its possibilities."

Nancy slid her hands up his chest and stopped at his shoulders where curls brushed his coat collar. "What kind of possibilities?"

One step closer aligned their bodies and his arms encircled her waist. "The possibility of a home of my own with you as the center of my world. I love you, Nancy. Would you marry me with all my baggage?"

"Yes, I will, Jeremy. I love you too, warts and all."

When their lips met, the couple could have sworn fireworks exploded around them. Soon the breeze cooled their ardor and they started to walk back.

"Come on, girl. I need to introduce Laura Ann to her new family member."

Hand in hand they strolled into the ranch house and stopped at the kitchen table where the ladies still sat discussing the next holiday celebration. Jeremy laid a hand on his grandmother's shoulder.

Laura Ann glanced over to see a gleam of happiness in his eyes. She patted his hand with hers and waited for an explanation of whatever had put it there.

"Can I have your attention?" Jeremy clasped Nancy's hand and continued. "I have an announcement. Nancy and I are engaged."

If the man had said that the moon was made of Swiss cheese, the group of friends and neighbors couldn't have been more surprised. Tears filled Laura Ann's eyes as she rose to hug him and his bride-to-be.

"I've always wanted a granddaughter to spoil. Now I'll have one," she declared with a sniff.

"Don't get all mushy, Gran," Jeremy said.

"I'll get mushy if I want to, young man. Will you will be staying in Centerville?"

"Yes, Gran. We love this country."

After a boisterous back slapping from the guys and hugs from the women, Jorge gave the other Bartlett sister an assessing look. Pete paused in his well wishes to stare at the riding instructor.

"You still plan to work here with us, don't you?"

"Yes. And I expect you to give me away whenever we get around to setting the date," Nancy told him.

The request seemed to unman the Academy owner and he hurried to the pantry to look for another bottle of wine to toast the couple.

21

The next three weeks passed in a flurry for the new wrangler on the Ridge Ranch. While the horses were being groomed, Slim got to know a lot about the owners of the Randolph Ridge.

Mitch was the kind of boss who worked everyday alongside the men he paid to do the work. And the missus, who looked like a fashion model, climbed into the corral with the Black like he was a Shetland pony who was too tame to offer any objection to her presence. As far as Slim could see, the woman was a regular horse whisperer. The Black would lower his head to nuzzle her cheek like a favorite filly and she would kiss his nose before she gave him his sugar cube. Slim was truly amazed at the camaraderie between the hands and the bosses.

As he went about his daily chores, he began to whistle a tune that had been running through his mind all morning. Da da da da, da de de de da da da da. Hum hum hum hum hum. Da da da da da da da.

José came around the corner of the corral to hear this vaguely familiar tune. Suddenly, the Ridge foreman recognized the song from last night's beauty pageant. A big grin creased his swarthy cheeks.

"If you break into a dance routine, Slim, I'm going to seriously worry about you." The foreman waggled his fingers in playful suggestion.

The new hired hand stopped to look at his boss. Arching one eyebrow at his fellow cowpoke, he struck a pose with a hand on one hip.

"You don't think I can dance?"

"Don't know for sure but you would need tap shoes and a short skirt not boots and rowels," José advised with a twinkle in his brown eyes.

"True enough but I forgot to pack 'em. What's on the work schedule today?"

"See that last corral of horses?" The foreman waved his arm in the general direction toward Centerville.

"Yeah."

"Time to break them to saddle."

"Good thing I had a big breakfast this morning."

"Yes. You'll need it cause it's gonna be a long morning," José told him. "Just don't toss that breakfast in my direction."

The morning was indeed a long one. Each horse had resisted with much tossing of heads and saddles as the ranch hands coaxed them into tame behavior. They were down to the last two who allowed the bridle without much ado but had bucked and snorted at all the cowboy's attempts to put anything on their backs. The foreman became aware of eyes watching from the corral fence. Turning his head, José saw the youngest Destchin brother grinning at them.

"What's up, Jorge? Is there something I need to do at the *hacienda*?"

"No, nothing there. I just needed to stretch my legs a bit," he replied. "Looks like you saved the best for last."

"If by best you mean the worst, then that is the case. These stallions are more like ornery ole cusses than young colts."

"Can I give it a try?"

José gave him a long look. "Sure. As long as you don't break anything valuable before you finish my house."

"No danger of that. I've been riding since I could walk."

"Do you want to borrow some boots and rowels?" Slim asked.

"Won't need 'em."

José and Slim climbed onto the corral fence and watched the young Apache approach the horses, blanket over one shoulder. The bigger of the two rolled his eyes at this new intruder but remained standing still. Jorge rubbed his hand down the satin neck and spoke to the horse in his native tongue. It must have soothed the horse's natural instincts. He nosed the arm of the man with a calmness that dumbfounded the onlookers. After a minute or so, Jorge grasped the reins and mane in his left hand as he placed the blanket on and vaulted onto the horses' back in one lithe motion.

José held his breath as the horse's head came up as far as the bridle would allow then began the stiff-legged hop and kick of back legs in a desperate try to dislodge the man who clung to his back. After about ten minutes, the horse stopped and turned his head to look at the rider as if to say, "You win."

Jorge walked the horse around the corral, stopping in front of the other men. He slid to the ground and handed the reins to the foreman.

"That was interesting. You should be able to put a saddle on him without too much hassle."

"More than interesting. It was amazing," José told him. "You ever think of giving up construction work? We could always use somebody with your talents as a wrangler."

"Not in a while but I will give it some thought and let you know."

*   *   *

Similar activity occurred on the White's Family Riding Academy. Horses were exercised, tack repaired, and the student bunkhouse stocked with supplies and a fresh coat of paint for the walls in preparation for the next session. Even with all this frenzied activity, Nancy managed to have dinner at least twice a week with Jeremy Taylor. They talked about all the little every day events that had occurred in their usual routines to check out how being together every day could be companionable on a basic level. It was the best way to gauge levels of interest.

The conversations weren't earth shattering but it gave them a chance to get better acquainted before the wedding date, which was set for the first weekend in March. Time enough for a honeymoon before the spring session began.

After a steak dinner one Friday night, they sat on the short bed of his Jeep in front of the bunk house looking at the stars in the clear Western sky.

"Do you plan on working as a riding instructor for a long time?"

"Haven't given much thought to anything else," Nancy told him. "When we first came to the Academy last fall, Diane and I needed jobs and a place to live after our parents died and we sold the ranch. This provided both and we like Pete and Gwen. They make us feel like we belong to a family again."

"I know the feeling. Even though my parents are good people, they didn't know how to adjust to my war wounds and the few friends who came to visit avoided making eye contact. My injures made them uncomfortable." Jeremy chuckled. "Taking care of Grandmother didn't let me brood about my own physical condition or dwell on the psychological effects they caused. Laura Ann didn't cut me any slack. I believe the term she used was 'man up'."

Nancy touched the long welt on his face with tender fingers. More of a caress than an examination.

"Working outdoors has made the scar fade a lot. Soon it will be barely noticeable."

"Yeah. But the ones on the inside are the most damaging," the veteran admitted.

"Then we have to replace them with more pleasurable memories."

Jeremy pulled her close with one arm around her shoulders. "Do you have anything specific in mind?"

"Oh, yeah," Nancy replied as she began to place feathery kisses on his cheek. "Does that help?"

The twinkle in his eyes answered that question as he pointed to his mouth in invitation. As Nancy covered his lips with hers, Jeremy slowly lowered their bodies to the bed of the Jeep, which was too short for the sexual maneuvering of bodies. Neither one had any privacy at their homes. The heat of their kisses made Jeremy wish for a softer surface. The metal ridges would cause bruises to tender skin. Drawing back from his date, he grasped her hands to still the passion rising in his blood.

"I'd better go before Pete comes to investigate with his trusty shotgun. Plus there isn't much privacy in the great outdoors or comfort in a Jeep bed."

"There is always the stable," Nancy suggested as she hopped from the vehicle and held out her hand.

Jeremy knew he should ignore the invitation in her eyes but desire trumped common sense as he followed her as she backed down the path to the barn with all that soft hay and only horses and one faithful hound as eye witnesses.

22

Grant Lord opened the wall safe in his office to remove the little square box that held his mother's legacy to him. He stared at the box for a few seconds before he snapped it open to reveal the solitaire diamond ring she had worn for the duration of her short marriage. Only sixteen years but they were full of memories of her smile and love for her family. Just before his father died, he placed the box in his hand and spoke softly.

"Your mother wanted you to have this, son. She said for you to save it for the one woman who was destined to be your wife and to be sure that you loved her faithfully. I only wish I was going to be around to meet her."

"Me, too, Dad. I promise to pick one who will be as good as she was," Grant had told him with a tear slipping down his cheek.

"Take good care of your sister. Don't let her browbeat you too much." With a crooked smile and twinkle in his eyes, Charlie Lord drifted off to sleep never to awaken again.

The horse rancher picked up the framed picture of his parents from the corner of his desk.

"Well, Mom, it is time for me to give your ring to my future wife. Betsy is just as feisty as you were."

He closed the box, slipped it into an inside pocket of his jacket then headed to Centerville and the jeweler's shop.

The ring hadn't been worn in over twenty years so it needed a cleaning before he gave it to his fiancée.

*   *   *

Peter White and his lovely wife sat drinking coffee at the picnic table early one morning when Grant Lord drove up. With a wave of his hand in greeting, the riding school owner invited his neighbor to join them.

"What brings you out so early on this balmy morning?" This question was asked with a derisive look heavenward at the overcast sky.

Grant gave him a strange look. There was nothing balmy about Montana in December.

"Never mind him, Grant. Would you like a cup of coffee?"

"No, ma'am. My nerves are already jumpy enough."

Gwen looked closer at the young man who clearly had something of import to discuss. "If you will excuse me, I have to put lunch in the slow-cooker."

"That was the missus way of giving us some privacy," Pete told the young man. "What's on your mind, son?"

"Well, you know that Betsy and I have been dating for almost a year and she accepted my marriage proposal unofficially when she was in the hospital after the car accident." At a nod of agreement from the older man, Grant continued. "As her father, I've come to officially ask you for her hand in marriage."

"As much as I appreciate the courtesy of a formal request, it is Betsy's decision to make. I know you will be a good husband and son-in-law," Pete grinned as he offered a hand to him.

"Thank you, sir. That takes a big weight off my shoulders. I even brought a ring with me today," he told Pete. "Is the lovely daughter of the house home?"

"Still asleep, I think but I'm sure she won't mind getting up early just this once."

A voice from the open doorway drifted out "No she doesn't. Who could sleep with those mufflers of his creating such a racket? Probably woke the rooster."

Betsy stood on the edge of the patio clad in jeans, sweatshirt, and soft half-calf boots, her normal working attire.

The look of adoration on the cattle ranchers' face made Pete rise from the chair. "I think I will see if Gwen needs help in the kitchen."

Grant waited until they were alone to catch Betsy's hands in his. "Sit with me for a little while. I have something to say."

"Okay. But make it snappy. The wind is a tad brisk this morning."

Grant sighed in resigned amusement at her remark. Depend on his lady-love to keep him on point. He pulled a small box from his coat pocket, placed it on the wooden patio table.

"I picked up something for you that the jewelry store restored to its former brilliance for me. I brought it back with me. Go ahead and open it."

Betsy eyed the square, velvet covered box a minute before she picked it up with trembling hands. She suspected what it contained but still she was surprised when the lid opened to reveal a square-cut solitaire diamond. The facets sparkled in the morning sunshine. A mist of tears filled her eyes as she raised them to meet Grant's.

"Betsy Edwards White, will you do me the honor of becoming my wife? Share all the ups and downs of ranch life."

"With great happiness, I will walk by your side forever."

Grant took the ring from the box to place it on her left hand then kissed her lips softly. He pulled her into a tight embrace to whisper in her ear. "We can celebrate properly later."

"Now we have to tell the folks the good news," Betsy declared as she turned to find Gwen and her father standing at the kitchen island. Pete gave her a hug while Gwen examined the ring.

"You done good, Grant. That is a beautiful ring."

"Thank you. It is a family heirloom."

"I thought I recognized it. I saw it on your mother's hand for years," Gwen told him. "It is too early for champagne but I have fresh squeezed orange juice."

Betsy hugged her stepmother and kissed the grizzled cheek of her father. "Orange juice sounds wonderful, especially if it comes with ham and eggs and hash browns."

Grant smiled at his fiancée. "I do so love a practical woman."

"Well, I figured you would need to feed those butterflies before we head to Centerville. We have one more stop this morning to make the announcement complete."

The cattle rancher nodded with a grimace on his face. "Yeah, I know."

Over breakfast, the ladies discussed the possibility of an engagement party and the wedding ceremony, of course. The men knew their input was not needed so they ate the food in silence.

"If you are ready to face your parents, darling, I am, too."

"Let me get my coat and gloves."

While he waited, Grant pondered the best way to approach the Sheriff and Mrs. Edwards.

Seeing the various emotions flash over the rancher's face, Pete couldn't resist offering a bit of advice.

"Make sure he is unarmed when you tell him your intentions."

Hearing this comment, his daughter admonished him. "Don't be ridiculous, Pop. Daddy is a regular teddy bear."

"Only where you are concerned."

Pete and Gwen waved goodbye to the couple then retreated to the kitchen for another cup of coffee. "My baby girl won't be living here much longer."

"Not to worry, Poppa. She will be here most days during the academy sessions and the Lord ranch is only a few minutes drive from here."

"I guess you're right but I've kinda gotten used to knowing she is under the same roof as me."

Pulling into the Edwards driveway, Betsy patted Grant's cheek. "Come along, love. It won't be as bad as you think."

"I hope not. Don't want to start out our marriage feuding with the in-laws."

Laughing at his nervousness, she clasped his hand and started toward the kitchen door. Turning the knob, she announced their presence.

"Knock, knock. Anybody home?"

The man sitting at the dinette table near the bay window turned his head to see his daughter and her boyfriend step into the kitchen. To the nervous bridegroom-to-be, the man more accurately resembled a huge Kodiak bear than the cute stuffed variety Betsy declared him to be.

"Good morning, sir. I realize it is a bit early for visitors and hope you will understand the reason why."

"I'm used to dealing with things on the spur of the moment so tell me what's going on," the Sheriff said.

"Well, I've given Betsy an engagement ring but we wanted to get your blessing."

Donna Edwards entered the room in time to hear this and squealed in delight. She rushed over to hug first Betsy then Grant. "How exciting! Let me see the ring."

While they were oohing and aahing over the diamond ring, Grant glance at the Sheriff who shrugged his shoulders.

"I guess that seals the deal. Welcome to the family, Grant."

The cattle rancher accepted the warm handshake as approval of the engagement. The butterfly wings stilled and he sighed in relief.

23

Today was the big day. The crew had put the finishing touches to the *Vargas Hacienda North*, the name that was burnt directly into the double wooden doors under the wrought iron grille opening of the courtyard. José stood on the paved walkway trying to grasp the fact that this land and new house belonged to him. Who would believe that a Hispanic hired hand lived here? Even he could hardly believe it. But by the grace and generosity of a cantankerous old man who treated his employees like family, it was his home.

Now it was time to get serious about filling the empty rooms with furniture. Not being very good with interior design, José had enlisted the aid of Kristy Randolph, his boss's wife, to pick out a few pieces for the living room, master bedroom, and dining room. The Randolph Ridge foreman climbed into his truck and headed down the road to pick her up for the trip into town. As he braked in front of the ranch house, Kristy kissed Mitch goodbye. He couldn't help but overhear their conversation.

"Remember, no lifting. Not even an end table," Mitch admonished.

"Yes, dear," Kris replied as she squeezed his hand then joined her chauffeur in the passenger seat.

As they drove to town, Kristy reviewed the list she had made for shopping. José had a hard time concentrating on her suggestions. Instead, he pondered the couple's cryptic exchange. The woman was a large animal vet who asked no quarter in her work on the ranch. Mitch was a devoted and protective husband but this seemed a bit over zealous even for his boss. José shook his head in puzzlement as he parked in the front lot of Wilkerson's Furniture Store. Once inside, they headed to the bedroom furniture section.

"What type of bed do you want for the master?"

"Not a clue. All I really need is a place to collapse at the end of a long day on the ranch. What do you suggest?"

Kristy gave the foreman an amused glance. "That depends on how many people you plan on sharing it with?"

The blush that darkened the Mexican's swarthy skin made her chuckle before she clarified the statement. "You might need a king-size if you anticipate a wife and a passel of kids who will want to snuggle up on weekend mornings before you have a leisurely breakfast."

"Snuggling sounds nice but I looked around at the dance the other weekend but didn't see too many wife options in town. Especially, when I asked if they could cook and tend house."

Kristy shook her head at his unromantic approach to marriage as she commiserated with the truth of this fact. "That's true. Maybe you need to visit the neighboring towns."

"Are you trying to play Cupid, Ms. Randolph?"

"Everyone should have someone to love and make them happy," Kris replied. "Besides, you aren't getting any younger."

Knowing he was losing this battle of wits, the foreman conceded defeat. "King-size it is."

Spying a rustic headboard, Jose motioned to it for his interior designer's approval. "Will this one do?"

"Excellent. It has a matching mirrored dresser and chest of drawers big enough to share. End tables and lamps will create a romantic ambiance." A wink from the woman made the foreman shake his head but the mention of end tables reminded him of Mitch's early warning.

"Not trying to put my nose in your personal business, but why is Mitch so concerned about your physical activity? You're not sick, are you?"

When Kristy's eyes misted up, he was instantly contrite and hurried to change the subject..

"Never mind. None of my business."

"Not sick, exactly. But women who are expecting a child have to be careful."

A wide grin creased his face before he enveloped her in a bear hug. "Congratulations! Another Randolph generation is exciting news."

"Yes. But we aren't telling anybody until our Christmas party."

"Mum's the word." José pantomimed zipping his lips.

"Thanks. I think you need a smaller bed for one of the other bedrooms for when your parents come to visit."

"I agree. Maybe, they have the same model in queen-size with a chest of drawers, end tables and lamps along with the appropriate mattresses."

"Now that we have that settled, it is time to check out sofas and recliners."

José and Kristy continued their furniture shopping. They wandered around the showroom checking out the model room arrangements. After much sitting and bouncing, they chose a mission style living room set with lots of colorful throw pillows, a solid oak dining table with ladder back chairs and a credenza cabinet to hold the assorted dinnerware they also picked out. The last things they purchased were three stools for the bar where the master of the house planned to eat most of his meals.

"That should do it for the immediate future," Kristy told the foreman. "They will deliver everything late this afternoon. That will give us time to recruit extra muscles to haul in the bed frames and set up the rooms."

"Thanks for all your help today. I was seriously worried that my house would look all hodge podge with me choosing the furnishing. I don't know how I can repay the favor."

"You're quite welcome. And lunch is sufficient payment. My stomach is fast approaching feed me time," she told him. "This baby already has Mitch's appetite."

"I would be honored to treat you and junior to lunch just as soon as I sign the charge slip."

While José was taking care of the payment, Kristy wandered to the bedding section to pick out several sets of sheets, pillows, comforters as well as towel sets for the bathrooms. Just one of the housewarming gifts that Mitch and she had planned. She asked the sales clerk to carry them to the truck.

Over a meal of very unhealthy burgers, French fries, and chocolate milkshakes, they discussed the upcoming addition to the Randolph family.

"El patron would be so happy to know that his and Charlie's meddling turned out so well."

"Yes. Even though Mitch and I resented their high-handed approach, they must have had a premonition about the future. Otherwise I can't understand James Randolph's will bequest."

Putting down cash to pay for the meal, they returned to the *hacienda* to wait on the furniture to arrive.

The rest of the day was filled with good natured ribbing as Mitch, Grant, and Pete helped José with the heavy lifting while their female counterparts hung blinds and filled the kitchen cabinets with pots and pans they provided. The new glass tumblers and dinnerware were loaded into the dishwasher for a rinse cycle to remove factory dust. By mid-afternoon, the house resembled a real home. José paused a minute to smile at the scene before him. His friends and volunteer movers sprawled on the new sofa and chairs in exhaustion.

"Come join us," Mitch invited.

"I'll be right back." José returned a minute later with an assortment of beverages. Beer for the men, sodas and water for the ladies. "Raise your glasses, amigos. I give thanks for your efforts to put together the accoutrements of civilization for me."

"Mercy sakes," Pete said. "Did you scan a dictionary for that fifty-cent word?"

"No. I googled it," José replied with a grin. "I salute you. Gracias."

A chorus of denadas echoed from the group who stayed for a few minutes longer then began to make their goodbyes.

"Time for evening chores," Mitch announced. "You can have the weekend off, José. Bobby Joe, Slim and I can handle it this once. See you at the party tomorrow."

José waved goodbye from the courtyard gate as his friends left then turned to look at his *hacienda*. A wave of emotion swept over him at the realization that all this was his and hopefully one day a family would be part of it. The sound of a footstep on the gravel of the road made him step through the wooden doors. Standing on the edge of the drive was a shadowy form of a person.

"Can I help you?"

The shadow walked into the light from the courtyard.

"Hello, Jorge. Out for another walk?"

"Yes. I do my best thinking that way," the youngest Destchin brother replied. "I wanted one last look at our handiwork."

"Your crew did a great job. If you ever need a reference on your building skills, I would be happy to give one."

"I'm sure you would and we'd thank you for that."

"Would you like to come in to check out the furnishings?"

"Not tonight. I'm seriously thinking about your offer to work on the Ridge."

José gave the young man a look of concern. While he wanted to use the Apache's nature horse skills, he didn't want him to burn bridges he might regret later.

"Have you talked this over with your brothers?"

"Not yet. I needed to decide for myself without their input," Jorge told him. "They think I am too immature to make life decisions on my own."

"When you do, remind them that a man takes control of his life even in the face of logical opposition."

"Does that mean the offer still stands?"

"Yes, it does."

"Then I guess I'd better get back to the Double L and face the music."

"Did you walk all that way?"

"No. I borrowed Tom's truck. I parked it at the end of the road. I don't like walking that much."

José chuckled at the man's honesty. "Let me know what you decide."

"I will. Goodnight."

"If I hear loud shouting, I'll know your brothers aren't happy with your decision."

24

The holiday celebration was a duplicate of the Thanksgiving meal except for the request from the hostess that they dress in casual party clothes instead of the usual jeans and boots. The buffet style food set-up would allow the guests to help themselves, even to seconds, without disturbing the rest of the gang's eating pleasure. The kitchen counter island was covered with all types of candies, cakes, and pies. A wide variety of side dishes were already waiting on the table runner that featured elves cavorting with livestock. Satisfied that their part of the menu was finished, the women opened a half-dozen bottles of wine to 'breathe' and put the eggnog mixture in a crystal pitcher for easy pouring. The pot on a warming tray held an old-fashioned wassail mixture guaranteed to warm the cockles of your heart as well as the blood coursing through that organ.

Gwen and Betsy had rearranged the great room furniture to make room for the enormous fir tree that the White family decorated the evening before. The twinkling lights made it seem like the limbs were lit from within with a wide array of ornaments. Miniature spurs, hats, six-shooters, and horses were a testament to the Western theme of the household.

"Time to put the presents under the tree."

The women had decided to have each guest bring a generic gift instead of trying to buy a dozen different individual ones. Practical things like gloves, scarves, thermal socks, and woolen hats, which were necessary clothing for the raw, winter mix known to fall in this Western state.

"I wish the Edwards family was joining us," Gwen told Betsy.

"They wanted to but Mom's knees were too swollen from arthritis to do any walking. Grant and I will drop in on them later this evening to tell them all about the festivities."

Even with the generic gifts the floor around the tree was covered with gaily wrapped gifts. In one corner at the back of the tree sat a huge bag filled to the top with what looked like Christmas crackers waiting to be pulled open.

Despite the cold temperatures on the patio, the White Academy owner, with much advice from the other males, was manning the grill from which came the appetizing aroma of meat cooking over Mesquite coals. It wouldn't be a Montana Christmas without steaks and pork ribs on the lower shelf and corn-on-the-cob roasting on the top shelf. A large bowl of salad with mixed green lettuces along with other fixings and rolls were all the sides needed for this holiday feast.

Soon the steaks were done to perfection and arrayed on massive trays in order of rare, medium, and well done as instructed by the woman of the house. Pork ribs with steam rising from the dish sat on the table runner ready for the horde of hungry males which included the construction crew who delayed their departure until after the Christmas celebration except for Jorge who was staying to work on the Ridge. He told José that Vitorio and Bonito accepted his decision because they understood his reasons, both professionally and personally.

The roasted corn had been unwrapped, the silks removed, slathered with real butter before they were stacked like firewood on several platters. Funky little holders were placed in each end to allow for eating without damage to fingers from heat and greasy melted butter. Pete strolled to the archway opening to announce that the food was getting cold.

The speed with which the guests abandoned the televised parade was more like a stampede than anything else. The men opted for the much used boarding house reach to snag a man-sized steak over which they splashed Worcestershire sauce. Only then did the rest of the food find its way to the platter size plates.

The two Bartlett sisters manned the beverage end of the counter and filled each glass with whatever drink the guests wanted. Soon the neighbors and friends gathered around the table.

Pete stood to salute them with a short message.

"Bless the food, Lord. Amen."

After that the only conversation stemmed from compliments to the cooks, even Pete.

"Awesome steaks."

"Wonderful rolls."

"Ribs are so tender they fall off the bone."

"No room left for dessert."

Gwen acknowledged the praise and suggested they open gifts then finish the evening with the sweets. Heads nodded in agreement.

Each gift had either a blue or pink ribbon on it to indicate male or female items. The gifts were presented to the gang with instructions to wait to open them until everyone had a gift in hand.

"Okay. Rip away," Pete declared.

Laughter ensued as some of the items were not only useful but comical, especially the one that Pete found in his box. A pair of red-flannel long-johns with a buttoned flap.

"Just the thing for running down to the barn for morning

feeding," he told the group who clapped loudly when he held them up to his body.

Every gift had been distributed except for the bag of cylinders. Mitch held the decorative bag while Kristy handed each person one of the items tied with both a blue and pink ribbon.

"Wait until each person has one before untying them," the horse rancher said.

With much anticipation, the Randolph's stood side by side. "Now open."

The first to pull the fat Corona cigar from the foil wrapping gave the couple a puzzled look. Unable to await any longer, Kristy broke the news.

"Put the smokes up until next August."

Only the women counted off the number of months this would be. Finally, Gwen smiled at them. "A baby, right?"

A beaming Mitch nodded his head in answer.

This got an immediate reaction from Grant Lord, who tried to get his sister to sit down in the cushioned armchair. Only when Mitch pulled up a footstool did she object.

"I'm not an invalid, just pregnant," she told her husband. "You don't act this weird when the mares are foaling."

"I'm not married to the mares and the foal isn't my child."

Grant approached with a blanket to place over her legs and received a stare and one raised index finger that waggled dangerously.

"Don't you dare act so stupid."

The rest of the men kept their distance from the ire of the expectant mother. All except Pete, who bent down to kiss her cheek.

"Gwen and I reserve the right to babysitting duty anytime you need us."

"Thank you," Kris told him. "If the eggnog isn't spiked, I would love a cup."

José hurried to the kitchen before the father and uncle could rock-paper-scissors for the honor.

"Here you are, Kris. I think the bombshell had the desired affect."

"Si. And thanks for keeping the secret."

"Denada."

Armed with plates of desserts and cups of coffee, the group of friends gathered around the den seating to offer prospective names for the Randolph heir.

Samuel.

Isaac.

Peter.

Joshua.

Michael.

Mitch, Jr.

Christopher.

"James, after the old man," Pete said.

"Randolph," suggested Tom.

"That would make him Randolph Randolph," Mitch told him. "And his nickname would be Randy, Randy. Not ideal for a horse rancher."

"Point taken."

José gave Kristy an amused look. "Maria is a nice name for a girl."

"A girl?" Mitch parroted.

"What's wrong with a girl?" Kristy asked with a glare at her husband..

"Nothing. I like girls."

"That is very apparent," his wife teased as she patted her abdomen.

This comment spurred another suggestion of names, each one more outrageous than the last.

Gladys.

Ethel.

Morticia.

Monica.

Daphne.

Hortence.

"What was that woman's name who dumped cheese sauce on your head, Grant?"

Grant and Kristy answered in unison. "Gena."

"Enough already," Gwen declared.

The hosts finally declared a moratorium on baby names and the guests said their goodbyes with hugs and kisses for the expectant parents.

On the way out, Jorge stopped Diane underneath the archway where somebody had hung a sprig of mistletoe.

"Tradition," he announced as he tipped up her chin to place a kiss on her willing lips. "Happy New Year!"

25

José smiled to himself as he reviewed the evening's entertainment in his mind as he sat in his truck in front of the Academy corral waiting for the engine to warm up. The holiday party at White Family Riding Academy was a rowdy Western success, especially after the Ridge owners made their impending birth announcement. It was one of the few times José had ever seen Grant Lord speechless. The man had even misted up at the news as he looked at his sister, surefire proof that the cattle rancher had a big heart and sentimental nature which he tried to hide from the rest of the macho men who made up his immediate world. It was a good bet that this child would be spoiled by everybody on the three neighboring ranches.

You would have thought this was the first pregnant woman in history. Both Mitch and Grant had tried to pamper her with all types of attention until Kristy leveled them with a withering look that boded retribution to the next nursemaid who offered to plump her pillow or elevate her feet.

It was comical to watch two grown men brought to a halt with just one shake of an index finger to prevent them from protesting the hands-off edict. Their outraged looks caused an outbreak of laughter from the other guests. Two strong men taken down by one feisty female.

After much friendly debate about names, Pete and Gwen

wished their guests a Merry Christmas and waved them on their way. Mitch and Kristy's obvious devotion to each other made him yearn to have a family of his own. He knew his house would be empty and his bed cold on this winter's evening.

Putting his truck in gear, the Ridge foreman turned down the pavement toward Centerville. As he tooled along, it seemed strange to be driving to his home instead of walking across the barnyard to the little house on the horse ranch where he had lived for so many years. so many years. First, with his padre and madre; then all by himself after they returned to Texas to take care of his ailing grandparents.

When he opened the *hacienda* courtyard doors, he saw a strange light inside. He knew he had not left any lights on when he went to the White's party. Surely, there wasn't a burglar breaking in this soon. Stepping out of the truck, he reached behind the seat to pull out a tire iron and closed the door with a soft click. The iron tool wasn't much of a weapon but better than nothing.

José slowly turned the knob on the front door and eased inside. He toed off his loafers to pad silently over the tiled floor in his silk socks. His heart was pounding in his chest at the possibility of confronting a thief in a physical fight but when he saw the object of the glowing light, he chuckled and lay down the tire iron on the hearth.

In the middle of his coffee table, someone had place a huge flower pot with a straggly fir tree planted in it. The tree was decorated with a few lights and one ornament that had a printed message on it. FELIZ NAVIDAD. A covered plate, a bottle of champagne, and a greeting card sat beside the tree. He unfolded the card and read the short note.

José,

We wanted you to have a "welcome to the neighborhood" housewarming gift from the Randolph Family. A Charlie Brown tree, a dish of tamales in the Spanish tradition, and a bottle of bubbly to christen the evening. Enjoy amigo.

All the Best,
Mitch and Kristy

It was nice to know that his extended family included such a loving couple to whom he could count on to make life interesting until he could fill his world with more than work, something that crossed his mind a lot lately. The love bug was in the air in this neighborhood and he hoped to catch it.

The foreman took the champagne and tamales to the kitchen. He placed the plate in the microwave. While it heated, he popped the cork and poured a generous amount of the sparkling wine into a flute. Raising it to the ceiling, José asked that this house and his friends be blessed this Christmas season. With any luck he might celebrate with a family of his own by the next holiday season. He savored the tamales at the kitchen counter as he partook of the first meal in his new home. After rinsing the dish, he refilled his glass with more champagne then took his glass to the living room and sat down on the sofa.

Looking around at the living room, José glanced at the furniture his friends had helped arrange. It felt like home already. He struck a match to the kindling underneath the logs. Within a few minutes a fire blazed in the fireplace to knock off the chill of the Montana winter; a feeling of contentment filled his mind. The furnishings might be meager but they made the room seem warm and welcoming. The rest of the design plan and wall mural could wait until he found a woman willing to marry him and fill the house with love and the laughter of children. Maybe a Carlos or Maria of his own. He let his mind imagine the future possibilities of this home and hearth. Lord only knows how long that will be.

Soon his eyelids began to droop. It had been a long day of happy endings for his boss and friends. Tomorrow would be another long day so José took himself off to bed. His sleep was filled with dreams of a life with that special woman, whose face was not visible in his mind's eye but who gave him all the love he desired.

CHAPTER ONE

The border crossing into Canada had been uneventful. The paperwork and passport he presented to the guards had even prevented the usual suspicion because of his ethnicity. Even in this day and time, he had to prove his loyalty to the country in which he was a natural born citizen. He could understand the caution but it still irked him to have people look at his swarthy completion and see only a possible terrorist threat. His blood might be Hispanic but it ran red, white, and blue.

José shook his head to rid his mind of this maudlin sentiment and concentrated on the voice of the computer directions he was hearing from the GPS since his eyes were a little gritty from staring at the pavement. The only other casualty was to the ranch foreman's back muscles from sitting for the two days it took to drive the Randolph Ridge Ranch truck and horse trailer to pick up the horses his boss, Mitch Randolph, had bought from the owner of the Knowles Quarter Horse breeders. The clock on the dashboard read twelve-forty-five. Since he had several more hours of driving, he began to look for a service station to top off the truck's gas tank. Seeing the all-night truck stop sign for the next exit, he decided this would be just as good a place as any other. He could stop to stretch his legs and get a cup of strong coffee, too.

The foreman slipped off the driver's seat to attend to

the gas pump. When his boots hit the parking lot, his first action was to flex his shoulders to ease the stiffness in his lower back. Pulling the ranch credit card from his wallet, he stood and breathed in the crisp winter air as the gallon indicator rolled.

After pumping the fuel, he grabbed his travel mug from the cup holder, locked the door then headed to the diner section of the truck stop. The Montana cowboy stood surveying the variety of goods offered before he saw the JAVA CENTER sign blazing over the counter in one corner. As he began to walk that way, the clerk appeared from the office behind the front counter. He removed his Stetson and nodded his head at the attractive woman.

"Howdy." His normal greeting was met with a puzzled look from the Canadian.

"Howdy?"

"I beg your pardon, ma'am. Good evening." The smile he directed at the woman was filled with the charm he used to cajole the female sex. It had the desired affect as she smiled back.

"More like morning, sir."

Her glance at the large clock on the wall which read one-thirty confirmed this statement.

"So it is. I stand corrected."

José continued his stroll to the coffee counter. Placing his mug under the tap, he pushed the button for espresso and watched as the dark brew trickled down. He hit the button again to get a double serving. As soon as the steaming hot liquid stopped, he put the top on the mug and walked to the counter.

"I'll take a couple of those chocolate éclairs to go."

The clerk placed the sweet rolls into a box before she turned back to the counter and punched the price of the items into the register. "That will be $20.75."

Even though he had cash, José handed her the Randolph Ridge Ranch credit card with his name stenciled on the bottom. He had to account for every miscellaneous expense on this trip.

"Is this ranch local?"

"No ma'am. It is located in Centerville, Montana, USA."

"Ohh! Does that make you a real live Western cowboy with spurs and everything?'

He couldn't keep a grin from appearing at her avid interest as she ran her eyes over his body from the top of his head to the tips of his boots. It was the stereotypical image gleaned from the movies.

"I suppose I am, in a manner of speaking. Do you know how far away the Knowles quarter horse outfit is from here?"

"About three-hundred miles," she replied as she placed the charge slip on the counter for his signature.

The ranch foreman scrawled his name, accepted the receipt, placed his hat back on his head then picked up the coffee and pastries.

"Are you sure you don't want to enjoy your coffee and dessert here?" A backward nod of her head indicated the open door of an office with a plaid sofa against one wall.

Another grin spread over his face at the unmistakable invitation from the young woman. "I really need to be on my way. Business comes first, you understand."

"Okay," she said regretfully.

He turned and walked toward the door.

"You come back to see us sometime."

The clerk's farewell made him stop and turn back to face her. The twinkle in her eyes meant come back to see *her*.

"That depends on how good the coffee is." With a wink, he touched the brim of his Stetson, pushed open the door, and headed to the truck.

The strong coffee had done the trick. He was wide awake

when he turned into the road with the sign that declared KNOWLES QUARTER HORSES. The clock on the dash read four forty-five. Not wanting to disturb the ranch house, José parked the truck and trailer in front of the red-brick stables. He left the running lights on then climbed into the back seat to catch a nap before the owners got up for the day.

His slumber was abruptly interrupted as a loud tap on the truck window made him aware that the sun was shining in the window. He sat up, flexed his back muscles before he focused his eyes on the slightly built wrangler who sat on a chestnut stallion waiting for him to exit. The hat and sunglasses didn't indicate if the person was happy to see him or not.

When he opened the door, the horse eyed him but didn't object to the hand that rubbed his nose.

"Good morning. I'm José Vargas from the Randolph Ridge Ranch in Montana. I've come to collect some horses."

The rider dismounted and extended a hand in friendly manner as the worn hat was pulled off to reveal a riot of brown curls that cascaded to her shoulders. Eyes the color of the grass underfoot gleamed bright as the dark glasses were removed. "Welcome to Knowles Ranch, Mr. Vargas. I'm Penelope Knowles."

For the life of him, José couldn't think of a single thing to say as he shook the woman's hand. His mind was too occupied with the pretty picture she made standing in front of him. Reluctantly, he released her hand when the woman gave him a concerned look then tossed a gamin smile at him.

"You're just in time for breakfast," Penelope told him. "Come along to the house and meet my father."

"Thank you." The Ridge foreman followed her silently because he was stunned at the sudden warmth that filled his heart. It was a ridiculous idea but he suspected he had just met his dream woman. As crazy as it might seem, he knew he would move heaven and earth to make her his own. Even as his brain absorbed this thought, he knew the thousands of miles that separated their worlds would make such a relationship difficult if not impossible. But José knew that hope springs eternal so he smiled at the possibility.

"Good morning, Mr. Vargas. I'm Charles Knowles."

The man who stood in the doorway was dressed in the normal clothes of a horseman but it was his manner that got José attention. Watchful waiting as he extended his hand to the Ridge foreman.

"Good morning, sir. I'm the Randolph Ridge Ranch foreman. Mitch sent me to collect the horses he bought."

"Normally, Mitch comes himself. Is something wrong on the Ridge?"

"No, sir," he replied with a smile. "Mrs. Randolph is expected to give birth to their first child any day. So, Mitch sent me in his place."

"And your wife was okay with you being away from the ranch," Penelope inquired casually.

"She might if I had one. So far, I haven't been lucky enough to fine the right woman." The look José gave the woman was full of hope and male interest.

Charles Knowles saw an answering expression in his daughter's eyes before she turned toward the hallway.

"Coffee and food are on the dining table. Come help yourself. If you want to wash up, the bathroom is the first door down the hallway on the right."

"Thank you, sir. I'll be right back."

"After breakfast, we can look at the horses and get down to *ranch* business."

Printed in the United States
By Bookmasters